# EVERY OTHER MEMORY

KAYLEE RYAN

# MESSAGE

Previously published in the Knocked Up Anthology

# COPYRIGHT

Copyright © 2021 Kaylee Ryan

All Rights Reserved.
This book may not be reproduced in any manner whatsoever without the written permission of Kaylee Ryan, except for the use of brief quotations in articles and or reviews.

This book is a work of fiction. Names, characters, events, locations, businesses and plot are products of the author's imagination and meant to be used in a fictitious manner. Any resemblance to actual persons, living or dead, or actual events throughout the story are purely coincidental. The author acknowledges trademark owners and trademarked status of various products referenced in this work of fiction, which have been used without permission. The publication and use of these trademarks are not authorized, sponsored or associated by or with the trademark owners.

The following story contains sexual situations and strong language. It is intended for adult readers.

Cover Design: Outlined With Love Designs
Cover Photography: Shutterstock
Editing: Hot Tree Editing
Proofreading: Deaton Author Services

# CHAPTER 1

Cadence

The beat of the music pounds through the speakers. It's so loud I can feel the vibration in my chest. Then again, maybe that's the alcohol or possibly the fact that I'm done. After four long, grueling years, I've graduated from college. Not only am I a college graduate, but I got my results back today. I passed my boards. I am officially an occupational therapist. It's time for me to enter the world of adulting, and I'm ready. I am so ready. I've busted my ass for this.

"Drink!" my best friend, Shelby, screams over the music. I nod my agreement, link hands with her, and follow her through the throng of people on the dance floor. "This place is on fire tonight," she says once we reach the bar.

"That it is," I agree.

"Two waters." She holds up two fingers when the bartender finally reaches us.

"I can't believe I convinced you to come out with me," she states, pulling me into a sweaty hug, making me laugh.

"You act like I never go out." She gives me a look that says "you never go out," and she's right.

"You were the most dedicated student I know."

I nod. She's not wrong. I put everything into studying—no time for partying or skipping class. I needed to know that I was on the right track to a career where I would always be able to take care of myself financially. Luckily, my nose-to-the-grindstone determination in high school landed me scholarships. Add in my part-time job at the coffee shop, and I'm not only a college graduate, but I'm also debt-free. That's almost unheard of—especially someone with my background. Hell, few in the foster care system make it to college. At least not the ones that I know. I, however, was determined. I *am* determined to make something of myself and my life.

"Now, if I could just convince you to find you a hottie to go home with, I'd call this night a success." She wiggles her eyebrows, handing me a bottle of water.

"You know casual isn't my thing."

"You don't have a thing," she counters. "Besides, look around you, Cadence. You can have your pick. You've got the eye of every man in this room."

"Uh, that would be you, my friend. Guilty by association." Shelby is what most men, even most women, refer to as a blonde bombshell. She and I are the same height at five foot six, but my hair is dark to her light. Her eyes are an exotic brown, with gold hues, and her skin flawless. Whereas my eyes are a light blue, and my complexion fair.

"Don't even," she warns me. A slow smile crosses her face, and it's one of mischief. I know it all too well. We've been roommates since our freshman year of college, and that look, that smile tells me she's up to no good.

"Excuse me." She places her manicured hand on the

shoulder of the guy next to her. "I was hoping you could help me with something," she coos. Yes, coos. The sound of her voice alone could have him eating out of the palm of her hand. "My friend here, she's just gone through a bad breakup." Lies. "He told her, well, let's just say she's feeling down about herself. What do you think? She's beautiful, right?" she asks him.

His eyes rake over me from head to toe, stopping a little longer at my chest, making me regret the spaghetti strap form-fitting tank top I decided to wear tonight. I knew this place would be packed, and if Shelby and I agree on anything, it's hitting the dance floor.

"She's a fucking knockout," the guy slurs.

"Thanks, sugar." She winks at him, drops her hand, and focuses her attention on me. "Told you."

"He's drunk."

"Drunk or sober, I'd take you home with me," he chimes in, still listening to our conversation.

I give him a kind smile, grab Shelby's arm, and pull her away from the bar, and to a small table that surprisingly is vacant next to the dance floor. "So, where's Matt?"

"Who knows." She rolls her eyes.

"Are you guys broken up again?" Shelby and Matt have a long history of on-again, off-again. It started our freshman year, and they're still doing... whatever it is they do. One day they're happy and moving forward. The next, they hate each other, and it's over. I live with her, and I have a hard time keeping up.

Her shoulders slump, and the look in her eyes is defeated. "I don't know, Cadence. I love him, but we're toxic for one another. I want us to work, but I just don't know if we're able to get through all the bullshit and make it happen."

"Maybe letting him go, I mean, really walking away for longer than a few days is what you guys need?"

"Maybe." She shrugs. "I wish I had the answer. I know he's struggling with football being over, and he's not going on to the pros like a few of his friends on the team. That was never his plan, but it's a huge part of his life that he's going to miss."

"Yeah, I get that. However, what about the last four years? He's always put you second. That's still going on now. There always seems to be something or some kind of excuse."

"I know. Now that we're graduated, I don't know where we're going."

Reaching over the table, I place my hand over hers. "You two will figure it out. Just don't hold out too long. I want to see you happy. Sometimes letting go is what it takes to make that happen."

"Yeah," she agrees when a shadow falls over our table.

Glancing up, Matt is standing there, hands shoved in his pockets, and a look more serious than I've ever seen from him on his face. "Hi." His eyes are locked on Shelby. From the look of surprise on her face, she had no idea that he was going to be here.

"Hi." The DJ slows things down a bit, and when he reaches his hand out to her, I know what he's asking. From the way her eyes soften, she does too. Matt never dances with her. Never. She loves it, and it's not something he ever takes part in.

"Will you dance with me?" he asks, his voice so soft I can barely hear him.

I watch as tears well in my best friend's eyes and nods her agreement. She takes his hand and stands before turning to me. "Cad—" she starts, but I smile and shake my head.

"Go. I'll be fine right here. This might be your moment," I tell her. The smile she gives me lights up her face before she turns and allows the love of her life to lead her out on the dance floor. Regardless of how distant he's always been, she loves him. Deep down I know he loves her too. I wish more than anything that they could get it figured out and be happy.

Not wanting to look like the loser sitting at a table all alone, I pull out my phone and begin to scroll through my emails. Shelby and I are moving to a new apartment, a bigger, better apartment, and we're waiting for our move-in date. After scrolling as long as I can, I head back to the bar for a drink, this time of the alcoholic variety. I am celebrating after all.

Moving up to the bar, I raise my hand half a dozen times and still get ignored by the bartender. Shelby never has that problem.

"Allow me," a deep husky voice says from behind me. Turning to look over my shoulder, I see a man with the most gorgeous hazel eyes I've ever seen. "What are you drinking?"

"Beer is fine, anything," I tell him.

He nods before leaning in and placing one hand on the small of my back while raising the other to get the bartender's attention. His touch is like a jolt of electricity to my system, and even though my back is the only place he's touching me, I feel him everywhere.

"Two beers," he says, placing our order. "So, you come

here often?" he asks with a smile as he slides onto the now vacant stool beside me.

"Does that line work for you?" I ask, not even trying to hide my smile.

"I'm not sure. This is my first time. How am I doing?"

"Meh." I tilt the bottle of beer to my lips, trying not to smile.

"Okay. All right." He chuckles. "I admit I need to step up my game. It would help if I spent less time working and more time doing… this." His eyes roam around the bar.

"You're not the only one," I confess. "This is the first time I've been out in, well… I don't really know how long. Too long, let's just leave it at that."

"Special occasion?"

"Kind of. I passed my state boards, so I am officially a licensed occupational therapist." It's the first time I've said those words aloud to anyone other than Shelby. I can't believe college is over, and I did it. I graduated, and I made something of myself. For me, life is just beginning, and for the first time in a very long time, I'm excited for what's to come next.

"That's incredible." He leans in and gives me a hug. His scent's something woodsy, mixed with the alcohol on his breath. It's intoxicating. "Congrats."

The hug surprises me, but I find myself accepting his arms wrapped around me and hugging him back. "Thank you. It was a long four years, but I'm done and ready to start my new career."

"So what's next?" he asks.

"I have a job lined up. It's local. I did my internship with them, so I already know most of the staff."

He nods. "I know you said you don't do this scene often, but what do you like to do for fun?"

"Well..." I can feel my face start to heat as embarrassment coats my cheeks. "I'm not much for spontaneity. If I wasn't in class or studying, I was working or sleeping."

"Ah, so this really is a celebration for you."

"Pretty much. I know I'm probably the most boring human on the planet, but my life... it's not been the easiest, and I was determined to make something of myself." I have no idea why I just told him all of that, but it's too late to take the words back now.

"Drink up," he says, taking a long pull from his bottle of beer. "We have some celebrating to do."

"Do we now?" I smile at him, and he winks. This isn't me. I'm not the girl who flirts at the club. My life has been hyper focused on graduation and my career. Now that I have all of that, I'm left feeling... unsettled, which is not how I thought I would feel at this stage in my life. Although I'm not much of a flirter, the easy banter with this handsome stranger seems to come naturally.

No harm in enjoying his company, right?

"Hell, yes, we do. You can't just sit at the bar all night. You need the full experience, and I'm going to give it to you. You and I are going out there." He points to the dance floor.

"I don't even know your name." It's my lame attempt at stalling. This man is too gorgeous and too damn tempting. My experience with men is limited at best. My first and only priority was to graduate from college. Now that I've done that, I'm not exactly sure what to do with myself.

Maybe this handsome stranger is a good place to start.

A slow, sexy grin pulls at his lips as he slides off his stool and steps in close to me. He's so close I can see the flecks of green, gold, and brown in his eyes. Maybe even a small amount of blue. They are the most mesmerizing eyes I've ever seen. Add in his dark hair, the five o'clock shadow, and the obviously toned body under that tight black T-shirt, and he's absolutely mouthwatering. "We're working on your spontaneity here, gorgeous." He smirks. "Come on. Time's a-wasting."

I don't know what the night holds, but I'm suddenly eager to find out. I quickly finish my beer and hold the bottle out for him. He takes both of our now empty bottles and places them on the bar, lacing his fingers through mine and leading us through the throngs of people to the center of the dance floor. It's a bold move, one that I'm not opposed to. He seems to have that effect on me.

We stop in the middle of the floor, and he moves to step in behind me. His hands grip my hips, and together we begin to move. I'm hesitant at first, which is odd because I love to dance, but this sexy stranger, he's got me off-kilter. It's not until Shelby and Matt appear in front of us, and she smiles, giving me a thumbs-up, that I start to loosen up.

"Feel the music. Feel me," his deep voice whispers into my ear. My eyes dart to Shelby, and she's swaying her hips against Matt as they stand in our same position. I mimic her movements. Closing my eyes, I let the beat of the music flow through my veins and just feel.

The beat.

His hands.

His hard chest.

Desire.

"That's it, beautiful. Let go for me." His voice is husky, and from the bulge in his pants, he's just as affected by me as I am by him.

I lose track of time as our bodies grind together on the dance floor. We're both sweaty, but we don't let that stop us from our hands roaming over each other. I've never been this turned on in my entire life. I can't believe I'm here with this Adonis of a man, and he's into me. Me, Cadence Wade, has all of his attention, and it's a heady feeling.

Across from me, Shelby motions for me to come closer. "We're going to go. You going to come with us?" she asks.

I'm not ready to leave yet and to be honest, I'm tired of being the third wheel on nights like tonight. "No." I turn to look over my shoulder to find smoldering hazel eyes. "I'm going to stay for a while."

"I don't want to leave you here on your own."

"She's not alone. She has me. I can promise you that I'll get her home safely," my sexy hazel-eyed stranger speaks up.

"No offense, but we don't know you," Shelby challenges him.

"I'm a man of my word." There is something about the conviction in his voice that makes me believe him. He's just one of those people that you can read, and I know that he's not going to hurt me or force me into anything. My gut tells me that this is okay. I can't explain it, and I'm not sure I'd want to if I could. There's something to this being spontaneous. Then again, it's all him. The man standing behind me with his arms wrapped around my waist, holding our sweaty bodies tethered to one another. He's the spontaneity, and yeah, I'm not ready to give that up.

"I'll call you when we leave," I tell my best friend.

She surprises me when she pulls out her phone and snaps a picture of us, then points her phone at my companion. "I've got this as proof as to who she was with. Take care of her."

"Without question," he replies.

Shelby studies him for a few moments before nodding. "Call me," she says, and I nod. I wait until they are out of sight before turning in his arms and locking my hands behind his neck. I don't say anything as we stare into each other's eyes. I allow myself to not think about what's next. Instead, I live in the moment, the feel of his tight grip on my waist, and when his head lowers and his lips hover over mine, I, Cadence Wade, do something I've never done.

I initiate a kiss.

Without reservations, my lips press against his, committing the feel of them to memory.

# CHAPTER 2

Trevin

Her lips are fire. Soft and sweet like candy as they press against mine. I need her closer. Sliding my hand behind her neck, I deepen the kiss. She opens, willingly allowing me to explore her mouth with my tongue. Gripping her hip, I hold her body close to mine. I don't give a fuck that we're in the middle of a club, damn near in the center of the dance floor. All I care about is this pleasant surprise of a woman in my arms and having every inch of her body pressed against mine.

When I came here tonight, I was just trying to get out of the house. I'm in town visiting my sister, who is recently married. The newlyweds kept making eyes at one another, and nobody wants to see all that. So I left. I told them I was meeting a friend and ran from their apartment like my ass was on fire. The reality of my situation is that I wasn't meeting anyone. I've been working my ass off for the last year, and I've lost touch with most of my friends, well, except for my best friend, who married my sister—the same one who was making eyes at her, and the reason I had to flee. I walked around town and ended up here. I told myself I was coming in for a quick drink, and then I'd head back. However, the minute I saw her sitting at the bar, I knew I had to say hello. I couldn't explain it if I tried.

Something pulled me toward her.

Now, here we are, her in my arms, our mouths devouring each other, and I want more. I can't seem to get her close enough. I can't seem to kiss her deep enough. My heart is beating in my chest, and my palms, I'm sure, are sweaty, but I refuse to let go of her to find out.

She's intoxicating.

When the song changes to Keith Sweat's "Nobody," I grind my hips into hers as we move like a well-oiled machine to the beat. I can't stop my hands from roaming over her body. My pulse pounds in my ears when she turns and places her back to my front, rubbing her ass over my hard cock. Bending over, she sways, her hips causing me to bite down on my bottom lip. It's been a long damn time since I've been this turned on. In fact, I don't know that I've ever been this worked up.

We find our rhythm with the slow, sexy grind of the song. We might as well be in this crowded club all alone because there is no one I see but her—just this gorgeous, enchanting stranger who's making me feel reckless and out of control.

And horny as fuck.

As the beat of the song transitions to another, my lips find her ear. "Come home with me." It's not so much as a question as a demand. I'd never force her, but I don't really want her to take the chance to refuse either. I have to have her. I need to be inside her. It's a need deep in my gut that I can't explain, but it's there, nagging at me, telling me that no amount of time spent with her would ever be a regret.

"Spontaneity," she mumbles, pressing her lips to mine.

"Spontaneity, need, desire, want, I don't care what you label it. I just know that being inside you is as much a necessity as breathing." Trailing my lips down her neck, I'm hit with the reminder that I'm staying with my sister. We'll have to get a room, which honestly, is better. I can take my time with her.

"I don't do this kind of thing," she tells me, chewing on her lip. I start to speak, to say anything that will make her change her mind, but she beats me to it. "But I want to with you. I don't know—" She shakes her head as if clearing the fog. "I don't have an explanation other than I don't want this night to end."

"Music to my ears, dream girl." With my arm around her waist, holding her as close as I can get her without carrying her out of here, I lead us out of the club.

"Dream girl?" she asks once we're outside on the sidewalk.

Turning, so her back hits the side of the building, I cage her in with my hands braced over her head against the wall. "You're my every fantasy come true." I give her no other explanation as I fuse my lips with hers. I let my body do the talking as I move in close, pressing my hard cock against her belly. Showing her precisely what she does to me.

Her nails dig into my biceps as I slow the kiss, resting my forehead against hers. "I want you."

Her chest heaves for breath. "I want you too."

"I'm in town visiting family. Hotel room?" I pull my forehead from hers so that I can gauge her reaction.

"I— Yes."

Sweeping her hair from her eyes, I make sure I have her

attention before saying, "We don't have to. There's no pressure. I can see you home if that's what you want." While I say the words, my cock throbs at the idea of never being inside her.

"No. I-I want to. This is just a first for me," she replies, looking down at the ground.

"Hey." With my index finger under her chin, I move her eyes to mine. "It's been over a year for me, and I promise you that you're safe with me."

"I believe you." She gives me a shy smile. "I don't know why. You're a complete stranger, but I believe you."

I feel ten feet tall and bulletproof from her admission. I don't deserve her trust as a complete stranger, but the fact that I have it has me wanting to show her she made the right choice. "We'll get a room, and we can just talk or kiss." I run the pad of my thumb across her bottom lip. "More kissing isn't a bad thing," I say, wanting to feel her lips against mine more than anything else in the world.

I watch as her fingers fly across the screen of her cell phone. I assume texting her friend, letting her know where she is. That's smart, and I'm glad. No matter how much she trusts me, she needs to be safe. Sliding her phone into her purse, she laces her fingers with mine and nods. I don't say anything. I'm afraid my words could make her change her mind, and that would be a tragedy. My heart thunders in my chest as we walk two blocks to the closest hotel. Silence lingers between us, but the electricity sparks as if we both could ignite in flames at any second.

It doesn't take long before we're checked in and I'm sliding the card into our newly rented room. I push open the door and motion for her to walk in ahead of me, with me following her, making sure to push the door closed and twist the lock, tossing the keycard on the dresser.

My eyes follow her as she walks toward the window, pulling back the curtains to peer outside. "Nice view," she says, her voice shaking.

"The best," I agree.

She turns to look at me over her shoulder. "You can't even see it." Her lips tilt in a shy smile. She knows exactly what I'm referring to.

*Her.*

"I can see everything I need to." I stand still, hands shoved in my pockets when all I want to do is rush to her, rip her clothes off, and devour every sexy fucking inch of her. But something holds me back. It's more than the fact that I told her she set the pace. It's— I'm not ready for my time with her to end, and I'm afraid that once I'm inside her, once our bodies have come together, she's going to leave, and yeah, I'm not ready for that to happen.

*Not yet.*

"I don't know how to do this." Her words are a whispered confession that pulls at something deep in my chest.

"We don't have to do anything."

"I want to." She looks down at the floor. My eyes follow her stare, and I watch as she steps out of her heels. It's on the tip of my tongue to tell her to leave them, but this is her show. I'm just the extra. The man who is desperate for time with her, to feel her skin against mine, to feel her heat wrapped around me. "I'm just going to need some help."

I look up to find those big blue eyes of hers watching me intently. My legs move on their own as they carry me to her. With my eyes roaming over her body, I take her in, memorizing that little black dress. There is nothing special about it—I've seen the same version on hundreds of women in my lifetime—but on her, on my dream girl, it's the sexiest fucking thing I've ever seen.

When we're toe to toe, I reach for the hem of my shirt, pulling it over my head and dropping it to the floor. Her breath hitches. The sound is blaring through the silence of the room. I repeat the process with my jeans, tugging them over my thighs and kicking them to the side. That leaves me standing before her in nothing but my boxer briefs that do nothing to hide my desire for her.

"My turn?" she asks. There's a wobble in her voice, but the firm set of her shoulders tells me that although she's nervous, she's in this. We're in this. Here. Together.

"I want to see you."

She nods and turns, giving me her back, moving her long dark locks to hang over one shoulder. "Unzip me?"

"My pleasure," I say. My voice is confident, but the tremble in my hands as I grasp her zipper and slowly pull until it reaches the small of her back tells another story.

I stand still as I watch her pull the dress from one shoulder then the other. She shimmies her hips and lets it fall to the floor, pooling at her feet. Black lace is all that's left covering her, and my cock twitches. With my index finger, I trace from one shoulder to the other, feeling her soft skin.

With a shudder, she slowly turns to face me. Blue eyes full of desire find mine. I cradle her face with my hands, staring at her intently, hoping she can see into the depths of my soul how much I want her. I don't mask the need that I have for her or the surprise that it's there. I've never in my life felt like this.

"Can I kiss you?"

"You better," she replies, and if she was going to say anything else, it's too late because my lips are on hers.

Her hands wrap around my waist, and I drop my hands, doing the same, needing her closer. My tongue strokes against hers, the taste of her exploding on my tongue. "So sweet," I murmur. I've never kissed someone as sweet as her, and her skin, it's so damn soft. I softly trace her back until I reach her bra strap. "May I?" I ask against her lips.

"Hurry," she says breathlessly.

And that's all the go-ahead I need.

I make quick work of the clasp and step back, pulling the small scrap of lace from her body. Her tits, more than a handful, are staring at me, her hard nipples, begging for my mouth. Not able to wait, I bend my head, sucking one into my mouth, making her moan from somewhere deep in her throat. As her nails dig into my shoulders, I take my time going from one breast to the other, lavishing them with equal attention, before dropping to my knees.

I kiss her belly and down until I reach the waistband of her thong. Gripping the material on one side, I tug, the sound of ripping fabric fills the room, and an audible gasp comes from the beauty standing before me. "Fuck," I murmur as I lean in and trace my tongue between her folds.

"Oh," she gasps, her hands finding their way to my hair.

When her legs start to tremble, I know it's time to move this to the bed. It's a struggle to pull myself to my feet. "Bed," I say huskily.

She moves to take a step and stumbles. I don't hesitate to bend and lift her into my arms. She yelps out her surprise but wraps her arms around my neck. In a few long strides, I'm laying her gently on the bed, stripping out of my boxer briefs, and reaching for my jeans. I fumble with them until I find my wallet and pull out my one and only condom. One. "Fuck," I mutter. Once will never be enough with her.

"My purse," she murmurs, her voice thick. "I have some in my purse."

"Thank fuck," I mutter, scanning the room for her purse. Once I'm in that bed with her, I don't want to leave.

Ever.

I can already feel it deep in my bones. She's got a hold on me.

"My best friend, she always insists we're prepared, but I-I've never needed them before." Her confession is soft, almost shy, and I find my chest swelling with pride that I'm the man she needs them for that this breathtaking woman has chosen me to give her pleasure.

Finding her purse, I hand it to her and watch as she pulls back the zipper and retrieves three condoms, handing them to me. "She was a girl scout," she says, shrugging.

"Thank her for me," I say with a cocky grin.

Placing the four condoms on the bed beside her head, I climb over the top of her. Her legs automatically open, allowing me to settle between her thighs where I belong. At least that's what this moment feels like. It's as if I'm finally home, and I don't understand it, and right now, I don't want to. I just want to be with her. I want to slide inside her and feel her heat. I want her nails digging into my back and her legs wrapped around my waist.

My lips find hers. I kiss her slow and deep, trying to calm my racing heart. Her legs wrap around my waist, just as I imagined, and with her feet locked, she's squeezing, drawing me in closer, my hard cock resting against her wet pussy. "Fuck," I swear, pulling out of the kiss. "You sure you want this?"

"I've never been more sure of anything." She reaches up and rests her hand on my cheek. "I can't explain this connection that I feel toward you. It's like I've known you forever, and I know I want it to be you. I have zero doubts. No reservations that you are who I want."

Who am I to argue? Instead, I reach for a condom and sit back on my legs, covering my cock, before aligning myself at her entrance. My lips seek out hers, and as my tongue slides past her lips, I push forward on one long stroke. I'm inside of her tight, wet heat. Her gasp and soft whimper have me pulling out of the kiss to stare down at her. The moonlight shows that her face is pained, and my mind slowly connects the dots.

"You okay?" I ask, my voice thick.

"Yes." Her eyes open slowly, and she smiles up at me. "Just needed a minute."

I swallow hard. "Is this...?" My voice trails off. I can't seem to find the words to ask her if this is her first time. That's impossible. She's in her early twenties if I had to guess and a fucking knockout. Shit, I should have asked how old she was. She's a college graduate, so I know she's legal. Fuck me. I don't even know her name.

Something stirs with the idea that I could be the only man to ever feel her like this. I've never been with a virgin, and never wanted to, but with this woman beneath me, big blue eyes shining up at me, I feel... possessive. I want to claim her as mine. Not just for tonight, but for as long as I can convince her to be mine.

What. The. Fuck?

"I wanted it to be you," she whispers her confession. "Spontaneity," she whispers.

"I don't even know your name." I give voice to my earlier thoughts.

"You're just passing through town. We both know this is a one-night thing. Can we just... finish what we started so that we can maybe do it again?" She smiles. She turns to look at the three condoms she pulled from her purse. "Maybe three more times?"

"You'll be sore."

"So worth it," she counters. "Please."

I've known her a few hours, and already I could never tell her no. Not that I want to. "I should have gone slow. Taken my time."

"I wanted it to be real. I wanted to feel the need that seems to be tethering us together. It was perfect. Spontaneous."

Leaning my forehead against hers, I take in a deep breath. "You tell me if I hurt you. If there is something you don't like, you tell me, and I stop. It's that simple."

"I won't tell you to stop." She lifts her hips, causing me to slide just a fraction deeper, something I didn't think was possible. "You feel too good."

"Fuck," I curse. My lips find hers as I pull out and slowly push back in. Our tongues battle as my hips thrust to a rhythm that has us both gasping for air.

"That... right there," she pants. Her legs tighten, just like her pussy as it grips my cock.

Resting my weight on one arm, I slide my hand between us, finding her clit, and with my thumb, I rub small circles. She's squeezing me like a vise, and I don't know how much longer I can hold on.

"Y-Yes!" she screams, and her body convulses around me. I feel the shudder run through her body, and that does it. I can't hold on any longer as I release inside her, in what will go down in the books at the best fucking orgasm of my life.

After we've both caught our breath, I kiss her softly before pulling out of her and climbing out of bed. I take care of the condom and wet a cloth from the bathroom to clean her up. Her eyes pop open in surprise, but otherwise, she says nothing, letting me take care of her. Tossing the cloth through the bathroom door, I climb into bed and pull her into my arms. As we lie in the darkness, nothing but our breathing between us, she has me questioning everything I've ever thought about myself. She's making me reconsider taking a job that will give me roots just to be next to her.

Over the next several hours, even with my protest that she's too sore, we manage to go through the three remaining condoms, and each time is better than the one before. As I finally drift off to sleep in the early morning hours, I know that I want to see her again. I've never felt this kind of connection, and I'm willing to do whatever it takes to keep her and the feeling of her in my arms and in my life.

However, when I wake just a few short hours later and reach for her, the bed is cold. Sitting up, I look around the room, and there is no sign of her, except for the condom wrappers on the floor and her torn panties that are lying under the chair. She must have missed them. Plopping back on the bed, I curse myself for not insisting on getting her name. My dream girl gave me the best sex of my life and snuck out like a thief in the night.

All I have left is a memory.

## CHAPTER 3

Cadence

Nine months later

I'm sobbing uncontrollably, my face is covered in sweat, and I'm utterly exhausted, but that doesn't stop my smile when the nurse lays my little girl on my chest after her first bath. My hand rests against her back, holding her close to me, and my lips press to the top of her tiny little head. She's bound up like a tiny pink burrito, and my heart is full.

I'm a mother. I have a family.

Sure, it's small, just the two of us, but we will always have each other. I will never let a day go by that she doesn't know that she is my greatest accomplishment, my greatest gift in this life.

"Mommy loves you," I whisper to my daughter.

*I have a daughter.*

*I'm a mommy.*

Sadness washes over me as I think about her father. The man who gave me this incredible gift, yet he has no idea. I never knew it was possible to be in the happiest moment of your life, but also feel sadness and regret.

I left like a coward that night because of what he made me feel. I was embarrassed to do the walk of shame and if I'm being honest, I had already fallen hard for him. It took one night, and I knew my heart couldn't take the rejection, so I left like a scaredy-cat. I tried to convince the hotel to give me his information, even offered up cash that I didn't really have to spend on my journey to single motherhood, but it was useless. They refused.

I've cursed myself more times than I can count for not paying attention when he booked our room. I was so wrapped up in our "spontaneity" that I stepped away. That's just another regret to add to my growing list from that night.

"We'll give you a few minutes, then we need you to try nursing her," a nurse tells me, bringing me out of my thoughts.

"Okay." I nod as more tears well in my eyes.

When I found out I was pregnant, I was surprisingly calm. It's not how I'd planned to have a baby. I wanted to meet a man, fall in love, get married, and then start a family —a family I never really had growing up. When I was nine, I was placed with my foster family. After jumping from one placement to another, the Gardners stuck.

The Gardners are decent people. They made sure I had a roof over my head and three hot meals a day. I always had clothes that fit and the supplies I needed for school, but there were no hugs. No declarations of a job well done when I placed first in the spelling bee. No, "we're proud of you" when I graduated high school at the top of my class.

They were detached. And while I still keep in touch with them—I send them Christmas and birthday cards every year—there are never any in return or invitations to join them for celebrations or the holidays.

The day I graduated, they told me I could stay until I left for college in the fall, and I haven't been back. That's not my home. But I was lucky and found that at college. Shelby and I were roommates freshman year, and we hit it off. We've been thick as thieves ever since. She's been my only family and listened to me as I obsessed over grades and my life plan.

However, life often has other ideas, though I'll never regret the night that resulted in me being a mother. Not just because this little angel was created, but because of him. Hazel Eyes as I've taken to calling him. He was my every fantasy come true. He told me the same thing, that I was his. He made me... feel, and I knew the score. It was a one-night thing, so when he fell asleep, I snuck out. I forced myself to walk away to avoid the awkwardness that was sure to be there when the sun came up.

When I found out I was pregnant, that wasn't the first time that I regretted running out that night. It wasn't the first time I wished I was still back in that hotel room, laying in his arms, feeling whole for the first time in my life.

As I lie here holding my daughter, who's not even an hour into this world, I worry about how I'll tell her about her father. I don't know his name, but I know deep in my soul that if I did—if I had a name and if he knew about her—he would have accepted her.

Don't ask me how I know, but it's a feeling, one that I will stand behind when my daughter is old enough for me to tell her about the man with hazel eyes who gave me the greatest gift in the world.

*Her.*

"You doing okay, Momma?" my best friend asks from the chair beside my bed.

"I'm good," I assure her. "Thank you for being here with me today."

"Are you kidding? There's no way I was missing this."

"You've done so much," I tell her, tears beginning to form again.

"Stop. You would have done the same thing for me. That's what best friends are for. Besides, as this little angel's aunt, I deserve the right to be here," Shelby says, giving me a watery grin. "Now—" She clears her throat, sitting up straighter in her chair. "Can you finally tell me what you're naming her?"

I look down at my chest to my sleeping daughter and smile softly. The moment I found out I was having a girl, I knew what I was naming her. However, I kept it to myself. I told Shelby that I needed to see her first, something I've heard other mothers say—at least from what I've read on the blogs I follow.

"Hazel. Her name is Hazel Marie." My voice cracks and my heart swells with love.

"Hazel Eyes." Shelby nods in understanding.

"Yeah. I took her father from her, and I want her to have a piece of him. That's all I know about him to give her, and Marie, as you know, is my middle name. She has a piece of both of us."

"I love it." She reaches across the bed and gives my arm a gentle squeeze. "For the record, you didn't take her father from her. You don't know what would have happened that next morning. You also had no idea that this little sweetie was created that night. You're doing the best that you can. Don't be so hard on yourself."

I nod. I don't agree with her because I will forever live with the regret of walking away. I was a coward. I was inexperienced, and the feelings that he awoke in me that night, they had my mind racing and my heart aching to never let go. I knew that wasn't what our night was, so I fled. I regret leaving, but I will never regret my night with him and my daughter. She's my everything.

"You sure you don't need me to stay with you for a while?" Shelby asks.

"No, but thank you. You need to keep living your life, and I need to learn how to live mine as a single mother."

"It's okay to ask for help."

"Oh, trust me, I will." I chuckle. "You're going to wish that you lived in a different apartment building."

"Never. I don't care what time it is. If you need me, you call me."

I nod. "Thank you, Shelby. I don't think I could have done this without you."

She swallows hard and nods. "So, is the plan still that Thea is going to watch her for you?"

"Yes. She's excited to bring in some extra income since Scott is the only one working. He insists that she raise Clint, and they not put him in daycare."

"Phew." Shelby fans herself. "That man of hers is intense, and finnneee." She drags out the word.

"That he is," I agree. "Thea's going to have her hands full with Clint and this little one, but she assures me she can handle it, and I trust her."

"I do too. She's good people. They both are."

"I agree. However, Clint will be four months by the time I go back to work, and Hazel six weeks, so she's definitely going to be exhausted at the end of the day."

"You sure you don't want to take more time?"

"I do, but I don't have the time to take. I'd barely started when I told them I was pregnant. I'm lucky they didn't fire me. My only saving grace is that they do offer up to six weeks paid leave, so I'm not going without money."

"That's going to be a hard day."

"Yeah," I agree, my heart already breaking just a little at the thought of leaving my little girl when I go back to work.

"Knock, knock," the nurse says. "Time to see if we can get this little one to eat."

"I'm going to take a walk. I'll be back." Shelby stands and leans in for a hug, placing a kiss on Hazel's head. "Love you," she says softly before standing and leaving the room.

With the help of the nurse, Hazel latches on right away, and as I watch her, I can't help but wonder if there is another way I can find him. Maybe I could hire a private investigator. Not that I have the money to do that. Sure, I make a good living, but I'm doing it all on my own, and babies are expensive. Maybe I'll start saving, and when I have enough, I'll try to find him. I owe that to both of them.

I want my daughter, *our* daughter, to have more than just my memories of her father. I just hope if I do find him, that my gut is right, and he accepts her in his life. I know what it's like not to have loving parents, and I don't want that for my little girl.

CHAPTER 4

Trevin

Three months later

It's been over a year since I've been home to see my parents and my sister. Twelve long months since I've stepped foot in this town. When I accepted the job as plant manager for the Lexington branch of Riggins Enterprises, I knew it would take me away from my family, but the pay and the opportunity were too good to pass up. When I visited a year ago, I was missing home and was ready to ask for a transfer or give it all up. After I woke up in the hotel room alone, I couldn't leave this town and the ghost of her memory fast enough.

That night still haunts me. Every other memory is her, my dream girl, who seems more and more like a figment of my imagination as time passes by. The memory of that night hasn't faded over the last year, which is what has kept me away. However, I can't hide forever, as my sister, so eloquently reminded me when she handed me my ass for not coming to visit my nephew. He was born around Christmas, and the family came to my place in Lexington. That was five months ago, and I've been summoned. I miss my family, so it's time to face my memories and stop being a coward.

The reality is, she was a woman I knew for a matter of hours. I shouldn't be letting her keep me from the people I love.

"You all packed?" Mom asks, standing in the doorway of my childhood bedroom.

"Yeah. You know your daughter, she insisted I stay with them for a couple of days."

"She's always been strong-willed that one," Mom says wistfully.

"That she has. I'm heading home when I leave her place."

"Well, try not to make it so long between visits. It's a three-hour drive from Lexington to Indianapolis." She gives me a pointed look.

"I know. I'm sorry. I let myself get lost in work. I'll do better. I promise."

"Good. Now you better get moving. Your sister is going to be calling and tracking you down, and it's about an hour to get to her place from here."

"I have a feeling you and Dad have been taking that drive a lot the past five months."

"Not as much as I'd like. We're actually considering moving closer."

"Really?" I ask, surprised.

"Yes. We want to be closer to our grandson. You know it would be nice if you moved home and gave us more grandkids."

"Mom," I sigh. "I'm not sure that's in the cards for me." A year ago, I would have shut her down, but one night—no, not just one night, the hottest night of my life with my dream girl—has me wishing for things I know I'll never have. Not without her. How she managed to ruin me in the small span of a few hours is beyond me, but she succeeded.

"I'll back off." She grins. "Just know I'm thinking it." She winks, wrapping her arms around me in a hug. "Love you, son."

"I love you too. Tell Dad I'm sorry I missed him."

"Will do. He wanted to cancel his fishing trip, but I wouldn't let him."

"I'm glad. He deserves a break. He's only been retired for what, two months, and he's just now getting out of the house?"

"Exactly!" she exclaims. "I get the place to myself. Now, shoo," she says with tears in her eyes.

"I'll come home more. Promise."

"Good. Love you. Give your sister and her family a hug from me. I'll be there to see them next weekend."

"I'll tell them." With a final wave, I'm in my truck and headed to the other side of town to see my sister and her family. It's long overdue. On the drive, I get lost in my memories of that night, the feel of the mystery woman's soft skin beneath my fingertips, the taste of her on my tongue, the way it felt to be inside her, and the knowledge that back then, I was the only man to ever have her.

I bang my hand against the steering wheel. I should have got her name. I should have insisted on knowing every little detail about her.

*My dream girl.*

\* \* \*

When my sister opens her door, I'm hit with the sound of crying. Not just from my nephew, who is in her arms, but from somewhere else in the house. "Come in," she says. I reach for my nephew to help her out, but he vomits all over her before I have a chance to take him.

"Shit," she mutters. "The second time today."

"What can I do?"

"He woke her up. Can you try and calm her down while I get him changed? I already called her mom at work. She's on her way." My sister is already headed down the hall toward her bedroom before the words are out of her mouth. Not that I can blame her.

Closing the door, I find my way to the Pack 'n Play next to the couch. Peering down, I see a tiny little bundle of pink, her arms and legs waving in tune to her cries. I've not had much experience with kids. It's limited to the visit from my family over Christmas when my nephew was still a tiny infant and didn't do much but eat, shit, and sleep. The cries intensify, and I know I've got to fight back the panic of not knowing what the fuck I'm doing and pick her up.

"Hey," I coo as I carefully lift her into my arms. Placing her on my shoulder, I begin to rub her back as I pace the room. That's what they do in the movies, right? "Shh, it's okay. He didn't mean to. Little man isn't feeling well," I tell her, and her cries turn to a soft whimper. "There you go," I tell her softly. "All better," I say as she shudders a tiny breath, which I feel against my neck, and her tiny body relaxes into my hold.

Something in my chest tightens at the realization that I was able to calm her down, and give her the comfort that she needs. Eyeing the rocking chair in the corner of the room, I take a seat and begin to rock her, continuing to rub her back. "Feeling better?" I ask her just as there's a knock at the door.

"I'll get it," Thea says as she walks back into the room with my nephew, Clint, and them both in clean clothes. "Hey, Cadence, I'm sorry I didn't know what else to do. I hate that you had to leave work."

"It's fine. I had a light afternoon anyway. Can I do anything?"

That voice. My body is frozen as my night with her comes rushing back. I'd know that voice anywhere. I've heard it every fucking day over the last year. In my dreams, walking down the street, in a restaurant, you name it, and my mind has made me think that it's her when it's never been quite right, not until right now at this moment. My memories and my present are colliding, and I know it's her before I even see her.

"Luckily, my brother Trevin showed up just in time for the second round of vomiting. I hope you don't mind. Clint woke her up, and I asked Trevin to help."

"It's fine. I'll gather her things and get out of your way. Is there anything I can do while I'm here?"

"No. I've already started my second load of laundry for the day, and Trevin's here if I need anything. Come on in, and I'll introduce you."

I know that in a matter of seconds, I'm going to see her again. My heart is racing, and my palms are sweating. As if the little angel in my arms knows I'm nervous, her tiny hand rests against my cheek, and my heart trips over in my chest.

"Cadence, this is my brother, Trevin. Trev, this is Cadence, and that's her little girl you're holding," Thea introduces.

Cadence, also known as my dream girl, the one who has consumed my every other memory for over a year is standing before me. My breath stalls in my chest as her eyes widen. She looks from me to her daughter and back again.

My wheels start to turn. Her daughter. I look down at the tiny human in my arms, and that tight feeling in my chest intensifies. "H-How old is she?" I ask, my eyes laser-focused on Cadence.

"Three months," she whispers.

I nod as I count the time in my mind. It's been exactly thirteen months tomorrow from the night we shared together. A night I'll never for the rest of my life forget. "What's her name?" I ask. My voice is gritty like I've swallowed sandpaper.

"H-Hazel." She clears her throat. "Her name is Hazel."

"Hazel," I repeat softly. My lips find the top of my daughter's head as I close my eyes and breathe her in.

*My daughter.*

There isn't a single doubt in my mind that she's mine. The look in her mother's eyes tells me all that I need to know.

*I'm a father.*

"Um, what's going on here?"

"Thea," Cadence says, her voice breaking. "He's, I mean Trevin, your brother, he's Hazel Eyes," she says, her voice barely audible over the thunderous beat of my heart.

"Oh my God," Thea murmurs.

"I didn't know your name. I didn't know how to find you. I'm sorry. I'm so sorry," Cadence says as tears begin to race down her cheeks.

Carefully, I stand with *our* daughter in my arms. I don't stop until I'm close enough to snake my arm around her waist and pull her into me. A sob breaks free from her chest, and I find myself fighting back the emotions of the moment.

She's here in my arms, and she's not alone. I have a daughter. *We* have a daughter.

Clint lets out a whimper that has me lifting my head to catch my sister's eye. She's smiling and crying as she tries to soothe her son. I never told a single soul about that night. No one except for Scott, my best friend, and I know from the look on my sister's face, he told his wife.

"Can we go somewhere and talk?" I ask Cadence. Such a beautiful name. It suits her. I also need to know everything. I want to hold her, hold both of them, and just... hell, I don't even know. I'm mad that she ran out on me that night, but I'm also mad at myself for spouting all that spontaneity bullshit. I'd known the minute I got my hands on her she was different. That was confirmed when I pushed inside her for the first time. I should have told her then that I wanted more than just one night with her. I should have insisted I get her name. There are so many could haves... should haves. But she's here. They're here, and we need to figure this out.

"I-I live across the hall," she tells me, reaching for Hazel.

"Can I? I'm not ready to let her go yet." Fuck me, but I don't know that I'll ever be able to let her go. This tiny little angel is a part of me. How do I walk away from that?

"O-Okay. Let me just grab her bag." She tugs out of my arms, and I miss her warmth. I want nothing more than to pull her back into my arms and kiss the hell out of her, but there are things that need to be said.

"Trev?" Thea says. I turn to look at her. "You good?" There are tears in her eyes, and a smile on her lips. Her husband, my best friend, definitely cannot keep a secret.

I nod because I don't really know what I am. I'm angry. So damn angry that I missed too much time with my daughter. With Cadence. With my family. There is so much swirling in my mind right now, I can't really determine which is stronger—anger for what I've missed. Hurt for the memories we've lost. Relief that she's here, that Cadence is within my reach, something I never thought would be a possibility. Disbelief that she's been living next door to my sister, for I don't know how long.

I've heard Thea talk about her friend next door who was unexpectedly a single mom, and she was helping her out, and it gave her some extra spending money. All this time, it was my dream girl and my daughter. My dumbass let fear keep me away when I could have been with them.

"Thea, do you need me? Need anything?" Cadence asks. There's a tremble in her voice.

"No. You two go ahead. But call me later." Thea gives no room for argument in her response.

"Will do," Cadence says before turning her gaze to me. "Ready?"

"Love you, sis," I say, not taking my eyes off Cadence.

"Love you too, big brother," she says softly.

I follow Cadence out the door and to the one directly across the hall. As I hold our daughter in my arms and follow her into her apartment, I can't help but think that this is my family. They're my family.

My mind is a jumbled mess. I hope Cadence didn't have plans tonight because we have a lot to talk about, I think, as I shut the door behind us.

## CHAPTER 5

Cadence

Fumbling with the keys, my hands shake as I try to unlock my apartment door. The weight of his presence behind me is a reminder of what we're about to face. What I'm about to face. The mistake of my past, not Hazel, and not him, but leaving him, is about to catch up with me.

"Take a deep breath," he instructs as he places his hand on the small of my back. The heat from his skin seeping through my shirt isn't at all unwelcome. After all this time, my body remembers his touch. The shiver that rolls over me is all the reminder I need.

Closing my eyes, I pull in a slow, deep breath and exhale in the same manner. Steeling my resolve, I open my eyes and manage to get the key in the door and turn the lock. Stepping inside, I hold the door open, allowing Hazel Eyes, who I now know as Trevin, to enter.

After shutting the door, I place Hazel's diaper bag on the floor next to the couch. "I can take her," I offer.

"No." His voice is clipped, and Hazel whimpers in his arms. "I'm sorry, baby girl," he whispers, placing his lips on her head. "Daddy's sorry." His tone's feather-soft as he speaks to our daughter.

My heart is thundering in my chest and feels as though it might explode at any moment. "I'm sorry," I croak out my apology. I don't know what else to say.

Standing in my small living room, I watch as he settles his tall frame on the couch, expertly holding our baby girl as if he's done it a million times in her short life. Shuffling so that she's lying in the crook of his arm, his eyes rake over her, almost as if he's committing everything about her to memory.

I don't move. My body is statue-still as I watch them together. It's not until he glances up at me that I move to sit for fear my knees will give out, and I'll end up a pile in the middle of the floor.

"Cadence," he murmurs my name. "Why did you leave?"

There it is. The question I knew that I'd one day have to face. I just imagined it being our daughter asking, not her father.

"I—" I open my mouth to tell him I was saving him the trouble and decide he deserves my honesty. "I was scared." I swallow hard, collecting my thoughts. Wiping my sweaty palms on my dress pants, I push forward. "You made me feel too much, too soon, and we were strangers. I told myself it was to save you time in the morning. We went into the night with our eyes wide open. I knew it was a fling. But with each passing minute, it felt less like a fling and more like... everything," I confess.

"If you would have stayed—" He shakes his head, and I can hear not only the disappointment but the sadness in his voice. "I missed this," he says, staring down at Hazel in his arms. "I missed you." His voice is so soft I almost miss his confession. Lifting his head, his hazel eyes bore into mine. "I'm angry. I'm so fucking angry," he says in a hushed tone. "But you're not the only one to blame. I'll own my part in this. I didn't offer my name or get yours, even though I wanted to. In fact, I had planned to. The next day."

"Oh, no." I cover my mouth with my hand to prevent my sob from falling from my lips. Not that it matters. My shoulders shake on their own accord from my cries, and there is no hiding it.

"What's her full name?" he asks.

"Hazel Marie Wade."

"Cadence Wade," he mumbles. I'm not even sure he realizes he's said it. "I want her to have my last name."

"Okay."

His head pops up. "Just like that?"

"You're her father."

"I'm her father," he agrees with a nod.

"Trevin, I'm sorry. I tried to get the hotel to give me your information, but they refused. It didn't matter how much I begged and pleaded or how many tears I cried. They wouldn't budge. I didn't know what else to do. It was just the two of us that night. There was no one I could ask about who you were. My only choice was to move on."

"What about her? What about Hazel? Were you going to tell her about me?"

I nod. "Yeah. My life growing up was… not one a child ever dreams of. I made a vow the day I found out about her that she would know what I knew about you."

"What's that? What do you know about me?" His tone is soft, and his eyes are full of intrigue.

"That you were a handsome man, who gave me not only

the best night of my life but my greatest gift. Her." I hold his stare. I promised myself and my daughter that if I ever crossed paths with him again, I'd tell him what that night meant to me. I'd tell him what *he* meant to me. It was one night, but my heart didn't seem to care.

"Tell me everything. Were you sick? I mean, women who are pregnant get sick, right? When is her birthday? How much did she weigh? I've missed so much. I didn't get to watch her grow inside you."

"How much time do you have?" I ask, wiping the tears from my cheeks.

"I'm here all weekend."

"I know you came to see Thea, Scott, and Clint."

"They'll understand."

I nod. "It's time for her to eat."

"Can I do it?" he asks softly.

"Yeah," I reply, just as soft. I stand and go to the kitchen to warm up a bottle and take it back to the living room. "She might not take it if she can see me. She's used to being breastfed when I'm around. I'm going to step out of the room so that she'll eat for you."

"You can do it if she needs...." His voice trails off.

"No. This is breast milk." I feel my cheeks pink from embarrassment. This man has had his mouth and hands on every inch of my body. We created a beautiful little girl together. I should be beyond embarrassment.

His heated gaze trails over my chest. My eyes zero in on his throat as he swallows hard. "If it's better for her to, you know." He nods toward my boobs.

"It's the same thing, but it's our bonding time. It's fine. You need this time with her."

"I don't really know what I'm doing."

"Here's a burp cloth. When she's about halfway

through, you have to stop and burp her. Make sure this is on your shoulder. She sometimes spits up. She also might grumble and fuss because she's a little piglet like that." I smile at my baby girl, who has her eyes on me just from the familiar sound of my voice.

"How do I burp her?"

"I'll be right here," I assure him. "All you have to do is take the bottle from her and place her on your shoulder. Then you rub or pat her back softly until she burps."

"Okay. I got this. We can do this, right, Hazel? You can help Daddy?" he asks, his voice raising an octave when he refers to himself as Daddy.

"I'm just going to step away, so she doesn't see me." I place the burp cloth over his shoulder and then hand him the bottle, quickly stepping out of Hazel's line of sight.

"Mommy says this is a piece of cake. Take it easy on me, yeah?" he asks, placing the bottle to her lips.

Our little girl is a champ, and enjoys her bottle and goes to town. I'm far enough to the side that she can't see me, but I have a clear view of the magnificent smile that lights up Trevin's face as he feeds our daughter for the first time. As quietly as I can, I move to my purse that I placed on the floor near the diaper bag and dig out my phone before taking my place across the room. I snap picture after picture of the two of them, all while wiping tears that are silently racing down my cheeks.

"Mommy thinks she's a photographer." He chuckles. "You're going to send me those, right?" he asks, not taking his eyes off our daughter.

"How did you know?" I ask.

"I can feel you. Don't ask me to explain it because I can't."

I wasn't going to ask, because I don't need an explanation. I have the same intuition when it comes to him, just like when Thea opened the door for me earlier. I knew something big was about to happen. I could feel it. I just didn't know what it was.

Never in my wildest dreams would I have imagined that my new friend, one who has been there for me since the day I moved in, would be my hazel eyes' sister. It just goes to show you how small the world really is. Or maybe it's fate? The universe's way of telling us that we were meant to be together? That's probably wishful thinking on my part, but I have to be honest with myself. He's been my one and only since that night.

"You're good with her."

"She's beautiful, Cadence. Her name. Is there a meaning behind it?"

I know he heard my hazel eyes comment when I was talking to Thea earlier. That's all it took was telling her that her brother was Hazel Eyes, and she was caught up to speed as to what was happening between her brother and me.

"Marie is my middle name."

"And Hazel?" From the tone of his voice, he's fishing, but that's okay. I'll tell him what he wants to hear.

"Your eyes, they follow me in my dreams every night. I wanted her to have a piece of both of us, and well, that's really all I had to go on that was appropriate to name a little girl." I smile, and he chuckles.

"I like it."

"What comes next?" I hate the wobble in my voice.

"Next?" He shrugs. "I don't know, Cadence. What I do know is that she's mine, I have no doubts, and I want to be in her life."

"Just hers?" The question is out before I can think

better of it. My already racing heart seems to kick it up a notch as I wait for his reply.

"You are her mother."

"You know what I mean, Trevin."

He nods. "I do, and honestly, I don't know if I can think about that right now."

"Please don't take her from me," I plead, my voice cracking.

"What?" The look on his face mixed with the tone of his voice tells me he's appalled at the mere mention of him keeping her from me. "Do you think that's the kind of man that I am? That I would keep my daughter from her mother?"

"I kept her from you."

"That wasn't your fault."

"I left."

"I'm just as much to blame. I didn't tell you what was in my head. What was growing in my heart. Instead, I curled up with you in my arms and figured we could figure out in the morning."

"And I was gone."

"The past is the past. I promise you I won't take her from you. I don't... I don't know what the future holds for us. I don't live here. Decisions need to be made."

The worry that's been sitting on my chest eases just a fraction. He doesn't want to take her from me, but what does that mean? We have decision to make? Does he want me to move? I've worked hard to build a life for Hazel and myself. This is the first true home I've ever had. I don't want to leave. Taking a deep breath, I decide I have to trust his word, and trust that we will work it out together. "Would you like to stay for dinner?"

"Try getting me to leave your apartment before I have to. Unless she's with me, I'm not going anywhere."

His words cause my panic to rise again, but he promised he wouldn't take her from me. The way that Thea talks about her brother, he's good people. My gut tells me the same—the same exact way it did the night I followed him out of the club and to the nearby hotel. Fate brought him back to us. I have to have hope that everything will work out the way that it's supposed to.

"Come keep me company while I make dinner. I have some photo albums you can look through." I made it a point to catalog her life. One, because I don't have any pictures from when I was her age, and two, I had always hoped the two of us would find our way back to each other, and he would want to see them.

With Hazel snuggled in his arms, Trevin follows me into the small kitchen and sits at the table looking through pictures of me when I was pregnant and every milestone our baby girl has surpassed in her short three months in the outside world. We eat dinner together, and Trevin helps me give her a bath, insisting on feeding her a bottle and rocking her to sleep. I hate losing that time with her, but I've had her for the last three months. It's his turn. He deserves this time with her as well. I just hope that when he needs to go back to work, we can figure this out. Being that far from her would kill me.

I send up a silent prayer that Trevin Hubbard is the man I thought he was over a year ago. I also pray that he remains a part of my daughter's life, and I might have maybe asked for him to be a part of mine as well as more than just my baby daddy.

## CHAPTER 6

Trevin

The sound of a crying baby jolts me from sleep. Sitting up on the couch, I lift my arms over my head, stretching out the kinks. A quick glance around the room in my sleepy haze, it takes me a minute to remember where I am.

Cadence.

Hazel.

*My girls.*

Crying. Something's wrong.

On my feet, I rush down the small hall and peek into her room. Her crib is empty but what I see just about brings me to my knees. Cadence is sitting in the white rocking chair in the corner of the room, Hazel in her arms. It's not the two of them together, sitting in that chair, that's affecting me, well it is, but not as much as the short shorts and sheer tank that Cadence is wearing. Or the fact that her full breast is bared as she feeds our daughter.

I don't know if there are protocols for this kind of thing,

but I need to be close to them. Both of them. My feet carry me quietly into the room, and I don't stop until I'm standing beside the chair. I lower myself to the floor and reach out, offering Hazel my finger. My little girl looks at me through sleepy eyes, but her grip on my digit is tight. Not just my finger, but my heart. If you told me a week ago that this little girl would steal my heart in a matter of seconds, I would have told you that you were fucking crazy. Now, as I sit here on my daughter's bedroom floor with her tiny hand wrapped around my finger and my heart, watching her eat from her mother's breast, I know better.

*This is love.*

Is it possible for my heart to be too big for my chest? I feel as though it could explode at any second as I watch the two of them together. "She's hungry," I say, my voice thick.

"Yeah. We're still working on the sleeping through the night thing," Cadence replies, her voice soft. "She's done it a few times, but this little stinker loves to eat."

"I should have let you feed her," I say, as the guilt washes over me.

"What? No, she would have done this if I would have breastfed her. She's a little piglet." There's nothing but love in her eyes as she glances down at our daughter. "You'll get it figured out, won't you, baby girl?" she asks Hazel, with a small grin tilting her lips.

The room is lit with a faint glow of a small pink teddy bear lamp sitting on the dresser. It's just enough for me to make out the features of the mother of my child. She's beautiful. More beautiful than my memories painted her to be. Right here, in her tiny pajamas, her hair a mess, her eyes tired, and her breast bared as she gives our daughter the nutrients she needs to thrive, she's never looked more beautiful. I know that in this lifetime, there will never be a moment that I will think that she looks better than she does right here. Right now.

*I need to touch her.*

Reaching out with my hand that's not occupied by our daughter, I rest my palm on her bare thigh, tracing small circles with my thumb. Our eyes meet, and that same electric current ignites between us. The same one that was there that night in the club. The same current that led us to a hotel room for a night of passion that changed me.

No words are exchanged, but none are needed. I can see it in her eyes. They're hooded, and the sleep is replaced with desire, and if I'm not mistaken, need. I see it in the way she shifts her position in the chair. She wants me.

*I want her.*

It's as simple as that. I can't explain it, and I don't want to. Never in my life have I met a woman who affects me as Cadence does. I don't know what it means, and tonight, right now, I don't care. All I can think about is tucking our daughter safe into her crib and getting my hands and mouth on Cadence.

All. Over. Her.

I don't have to wonder if she wants the same thing because when my eyes meet hers, her breath hitches. My cock stirs as the memories of our time together replay in my mind. This is nothing new for me. I'm not ashamed to admit that I've taken matters into my own hands, literally, at the memory of that night. Now, here she is sitting before me with a piece of the two of us in her arms.

With each passing minute, the anger fades, and something else takes its place. That something causes a flutter in my chest. I'm as much to blame as she is. "We used protection," I say out loud. "That night, we used protection."

"We did. Every time."

"Then how did we get this little angel?" I ask, nodding toward Hazel, whose eyes are growing heavy as her belly gets full.

"Condoms are not 100 percent effective."

"Were you not on the pill?" I realize as I ask the question that we should have had this conversation that night, but I was too wrapped up in her and the indescribable connection to worry about the specifics. I suited up. I thought we were good. "Sorry," I say when I realize how my question sounded. "I'm just thinking out loud. I don't blame you, Cadence." Her name rolls off my tongue like a caress.

"No. I'm not on the pill," she answers. "I wasn't sleeping with anyone. I hadn't," she adds, and I kid you not, my cock aches at the memory of knowing that I'm the only man who's ever been inside of her. Well, I was the first.

"And now?"

"No. I'm not— I mean, Hazel is my priority."

"Has there been anyone since me?" I toss the question out there. Partly because I'm curious, and the other part knows that not knowing will eat me alive until I have the answer.

"No." Her voice is barely audible, but in the silence of the room, I hear her loud and clear. "W-What about you?"

"No. However, that's not from my lack of trying. I tried random hookups a few times and never made it past a kiss or two. They didn't taste like you," I say, leaning in and pressing my lips to her bare thigh. "They didn't smell like you. You've ruined me." There hasn't been a woman in my life who could compare to her since that night. Hell, there has never in my life been a woman who has compared to her, and I know as I sit here looking up at her, that there never will.

"I need to lay her down," she says. Her voice is soft, but

I still hear the vulnerability as she speaks. We're both on a road less traveled. We've made it to the fork in the road, and we need to decide our path.

I watch as she stands with our daughter in her arms and carries her to her crib. She places her back on the small mattress and quickly covers herself, much to my dismay. My eyes are glued to Cadence as I watch her kiss the tips of her index and middle fingers and place them on our daughter's forehead.

"Mommy and Daddy love you," she whispers, and my heart stops.

"C-Cadence?" She turns to look at me. "Do—" I swallow hard. "Do you tell her that every night?"

"Tell her what?" She tilts her head to the side, and I want nothing more than to trace the slender column of her neck with my lips, but I need to hear her answer first.

"That Mommy and Daddy love her."

"Oh." She places her hand over her mouth, and tears well in her eyes. "I'm sorry. It's a habit, and I know you can tell her now on your own, but I wanted her to know that she was loved, and I knew... something in my gut told me that if you knew about her, you would be in her life, and well, I didn't have the best childhood. I never wanted her to wonder if she was loved." She opens her mouth to say something else, but I'm faster. My hand slides behind her neck, and I pull her lips to mine. I kiss her hard as the emotions of her confession wash over me.

At this moment, with our lips pressed together, there is no time between us. No missed moments. It's just the two of us and the passion that we can't deny. It doesn't matter that she left, and it doesn't matter that I should have told her that it meant more to me than just a night of fun. We've both made mistakes, but I don't want to live in the past. I want to live in the present, with a future that involves the two of us and our baby girl. It's as if no time has passed as our tongues collide.

"I want you," I whisper against her lips.

"Bedroom."

Not needing any further invitation, I lift her in my arms and carry her across the hall to her bedroom. As soon as her feet hit the floor, she's raising her arms in the air. I waste no time pulling the small tank over her head, allowing her full breasts to spill out. My mouth waters needing them in my mouth. Bending my head, I suck one hard nipple gently into my mouth. Cadence moans, burying her hands in my hair. With the pad of my thumb, I trace the other, giving it equal attention.

"That's good," she moans. "So sensitive."

"Am I hurting you?" I pull back just far enough to ask.

"No. No. No, don't stop," she says, panicked.

"Don't worry, baby. I'm just getting started," I assure her, before dropping to my knees and helping her out of the tiny boy shorts she's wearing.

"Trevin." There's something in her voice that has me looking up at her, giving her my full attention. "I'm not— I mean my body. It's different now," she says with a wobble of worry in her voice. From the glow of the bedside lamp, I can see the rosy color of embarrassment on her cheeks. Then again, that might be desire. I can't be sure.

My lips kiss just above her pelvic bone over the pale red stretch mark. "You mean the body that grew and created our daughter? The body that gave her life and still nurtures her. Your body is different, Cadence, but it's sexy as fuck. I wish I could have seen you. I wish I could have cradled Hazel when she rested here." My hand roams over her belly. "I wish I could have seen your body grow and change with our daughter." Resting my forehead against her belly, I wrap my arms around Cadence and hold her tight. The enormity of what I've missed catches up to me. Those are memories I'll never have.

I won't let the same mistake happen twice. We were both responsible for our pasts, but we are the ones who decide our future. I'm determined never to miss another chance for a memory with either of them. I feel her hands in my hair, and when I peer up at her, I see the silent tears rolling down her cheeks. The sight breaks my heart open. I need her to know, need her to understand that I'm in this. That I'm not going anywhere, and if I do, they're coming with me.

Standing, I cradle her face in the palm of my hands. "I'm here, Cadence. I'm here, and this is exactly where I want to be. I'm not leaving you. I'm not leaving her. I don't know what that looks like. There are so many things that we're going to have to work out, but I want you." I stare deep into her eyes, willing her to believe me. "I want both of you."

Moving to stand on the tip of her toes, she presses her lips to mine. I can taste the saltiness of her tears, but that doesn't stop me from tracing her lips with my tongue. I could kiss her like this every day for the rest of my life, and it wouldn't be enough. No amount of time with her will ever be enough. When we finally come up for air, I grip her hips and toss her on the bed. She bounces a few times as the sound of her laughter fills the room.

"Is she a light sleeper?" I ask.

"Not at all. I read a book that said to keep doing normal household chores so that the baby will be used to sleeping through noises. We won't wake her up."

"Don't move a muscle. I'll be right back." Rushing out of

the room and down the hall, I grab my wallet from the coffee table and pull out the single condom that has been there for months. Not wasting time, I head back to her room and hold it up. "It's been in my wallet for a few months." I walk toward the lamp so that I can see the expiration date. "But it's still good."

Cadence shrugs. "It didn't work out so well for us the first time."

"What are you saying?"

"Just that they're not 100 percent."

"You telling me I can go bare?" I ask, my voice thick at the mere thought.

"Hazel isn't ready for a sibling just yet."

"But if it fails?"

She shrugs. "Then, she gets to be a big sister sooner than later."

I nod. What I don't say is that I would be perfectly fine with another baby. Fuck me. I want a house full of tiny humans that we create. I'm not a man who's said he's never getting married and didn't want kids. I've just never found a woman I wanted to spend every day of forever with.

Until now.

Now I have two ladies in my life that I'm going to hold onto with everything I have and never let go. After ripping open the condom, I slide it over my length and climb onto the bed, settling where I belong—between her thighs. "We only have one. Unless...." I let the unfinished question hang between us.

"Then we're going to have to make it count," she says, draping her arms over my shoulders.

"We are definitely going to make it count." My lips press to hers, and I do exactly that.

## CHAPTER 7

Cadence

A crash from somewhere in the apartment wakes me up. I still and listen but hear nothing. Glancing at the clock, I see it's after eight, and I never sleep this late. Hazel never sleeps this late. *Shit. Hazel.* I jump out of bed and race to her room. She's not there. A deep throaty voice comes from the living room, and I follow the sound. Last night comes rushing back to me. Trevin "Hazel Eyes" is here. I tug at the hem of his T-shirt that I'm wearing, and the memory of him moving inside me causes my body to heat.

My racing heart slows as my mind realizes that it's Trevin in my apartment with our daughter. Peeking around the corner, I see him sitting on the couch with Hazel in his arms. He's shirtless, wearing nothing but his boxer briefs, with a burp cloth tossed over his toned shoulder.

"Daddy's not too good at this yet, pumpkin. You need to bear with me. I promise I'll learn how to take care of you. I watched Mommy do this yesterday and I think I've got it."

He tests a small drop of the bottle on his wrist. "I read this online last night that I should test the temperature here. I guess if Mommy was feeding you, we wouldn't have to worry about that."

He offers Hazel her bottle, and she takes it without issue. I can hear her gulps from here. Trevin smiles down at her, and there is nothing but love in his eyes.

"Morning, beautiful," he says, looking up at me. "You going to come and join us?" He nods to the empty cushion next to them on the couch.

I don't waste any time walking further into the room to take the offered seat. "Hey, sweet girl." I lean over and kiss my daughter on the forehead. I expect her to want me, but she just grins around her bottle and goes back to eating.

"I think she likes me." Trevin smiles.

"I'd say she more than likes you. You're her daddy. I think she knows that."

"Really?" The insecurity in that one single word has me reassuring him.

"Absolutely. Babies are smart, and it helps that you treat her like she's your world."

"She is." He looks over at me. "You both are."

"Trev—" I start, but he stops me.

"No. Let me finish. That night, I wanted to wake up with you the next day and tell you I wanted to see you again. I knew that the one night was never enough. I didn't know how we were going to make it happen, just that I wanted to. Sitting here with the two of you... the last twenty-four hours have been more than I could have hoped for. I want you in my life. I want to be in her life and in yours. I know it's soon, but I feel it deep."

"Sounds like a fairy tale."

"It is, baby. It's our fairy tale. I want to live it out with you." He looks down at Hazel. "Regardless of what happens between us, I have some changes I need to make. I need to find a job and put my place on the market, find a new place here."

"What? You're just uprooting your life?"

"You're here. She's here. My family is here."

"But your job, your life is in Lexington."

"That's where you're wrong. My life is in the apartment. My girls." He leans over and places a kiss on my temple. My heart skips a beat as I will his words to be true.

Before I can reply, there's a knock at the door. Standing, I go to answer it. "Hey," I greet Thea. I'm nervous standing before my best friend. How will my relationship with her brother affect our friendship? How will she react to actually being Hazel's aunt, not just an honorary title we've given her?

She looks at Trevin's shirt I'm wearing, that thankfully comes to just above my knees. "I see things went well," she states.

"We're a work in progress," I tell her. That's not exactly true, but this is his sister, and I don't know what he wants her to know and not know. It's difficult because she's become one of my closest friends.

"We're a family," Trevin says from behind me.

I turn to look at him, and he's standing with Hazel pressed against his chest and shoulder, rubbing her back.

"Come on, Trev, I don't need to see all that." Thea pretends to gag and shield her eyes from her brother. However, I didn't miss the soft expression in her eyes at seeing him holding his daughter. Our daughter.

"Then don't come knocking on my girl's door first thing in the morning," he fires back.

"Your girl, huh?" she asks, amused.

"My girls," he corrects. He steps closer to me, and slides the arm not holding Hazel around my waist. I step into his embrace, loving the feel of being in his arms. Loving that we're his girls.

"What are the two of you doing later? I thought we could maybe take the kids to the aquarium."

"Babe?" Trevin looks to me.

"Um... yeah, if you want."

"What time?" Trevin asks his sister.

"Around noon? That will be after morning naps, and both kids will have full bellies," she comments.

"Good point," I agree with her.

"We'll meet you there," Trevin says. "Now, let me get back to my family, and you need to get back to yours."

"You do remember that I'm your sister, right?"

"Yes. And I love you, but I just got them, Thea."

Tears well in Thea's eyes. "I love you." She leans in for a hug. "And you," she says, turning to look at me once she's released him. "How have I gone all this time and not realized it was my big brother?"

I too have tears in my eyes. "Because I didn't have a name. I didn't know where he was from, just that he was visiting."

"But Hazel Eyes. I should have connected the dots."

"Why would you? There are millions of men with hazel eyes."

"Yeah," she concedes. "You good?" From the soft tone of her voice, I know she's not asking as my daughter's aunt, but as my friend.

"We're good."

She turns and points at her brother. "Don't be late."

"Then leave so I can finish feeding my daughter and

work on feeding her mother." He wags his eyebrows, and Thea, although laughing, pretends to gag.

"I could have gone without that," she says, opening the door and stepping into the hall.

"Love you, little sister," Trevin says, closing the door. "I have to give her hell because she's my little sister, but I'm so fucking glad that she was the one watching Hazel."

"She's amazing, and she's been a huge help to me with Hazel. She was there for me while I was pregnant and during and after delivery. She and my best friend, Shelby. I couldn't have done any of this without them."

"I doubt that. You're an amazing mother."

"You don't know that."

"Bullshit. I see how happy Hazel is. She's healthy, and you came right away yesterday. You're the best momma this little angel could ask for. Her daddy too."

"You got her?" I ask, changing the subject. I still feel a mound of guilt resting on my shoulders, that due to my actions, Hazel lost time with her daddy. Sure, she'll never remember, but one day she's going to ask why he was never in any of my pregnancy photos, or photos of her the first three months of her life. I'm going to have to answer for that. "I'm going to make us some breakfast."

"I wanted to have you for breakfast." He smirks.

"No condoms," I remind him.

"Don't need them for what I have planned." The devilish smile tilting his lips tells me exactly what that is.

A shiver of anticipation races down my spine. "Real food first, and then we'll see."

Snaking an arm around my waist, he pulls me into him and presses his lips to mine. "It's going to happen, baby. I promise you that." He smacks my ass and struts back to the living room to finish giving Hazel the rest of her breakfast. I can't help but wonder how this is my life.

\* \* \*

It turns out I had a hard time pulling Trevin away from Hazel. He insisted he hold her while we ate our own breakfast. He played with her until she was too fussy to keep going. She was a handful as he tried to get her to sleep, but he insisted that he could do it. My mom instincts told me to just take her from him, but then I reminded myself that he is her father. More importantly, he's here and wants to help take care of her. He wants to learn our routine, what she likes, and what she doesn't. How do I get in the way of that?

"I have to admit," Trevin says, coming back to the living after laying Hazel in her crib. "I wasn't sure I was going to be successful at getting her to sleep."

"She fights it sometimes. My guess is that she was having too much fun playing with you, and she didn't want to miss it."

"Yeah?" His eyes light up.

"Yes."

"I love her, Cadence." He shakes his head, and the look on his face tells me that he's in disbelief. "I never thought—" He smiles. "She's perfect."

"She is. She's such a good baby."

"You've done an incredible job with her. Thank you. I know it was hard for you to do it all on your own. I'm sorry I wasn't here for both of you."

"It was unavoidable. The past is behind us."

"Moving forward," he says, offering me his hand. "I believe I made you a promise."

"I'm not going to hold you to that. We really need to get ready."

"We have time," he says, not bothering to glance at the clock. His phone rings, and he grins when he looks at the screen. "Hey, Mom."

I freeze when I hear the word "Mom" come out of his mouth. My attention is focused on him as I wait to see what's going to happen. Will he tell her about Hazel? About me? My hands grip the hem of his T-shirt that I'm still wearing to keep from wringing them together. Will they hate me? Will they accept her? There are so many questions filtering through my mind.

"Oh, she did, did she?" He grins. "Yeah, I do have some news. Hold on, let me switch to video, and I'll show you."

I shriek and take off, running down the hall. His laughter follows me. "That was Cadence," he explains. "She's special." I hear him tell his mother.

I'm in my bedroom with my ear pressed to the door. I'm not ashamed to be listening to his conversation. I would have remained out in the living room, but the last thing his mom needs to see when she meets me for the first time, via video or in person, is me in her son's T-shirt sans bra, and my hair a mess from our lovemaking the night before.

That's a hard pass for me.

I'm sure it's going to be a hard-enough battle when she finds out I kept Hazel from him, even though it was beyond my control. I'm glad Thea understands the entire story. She knows how the night went down. I hate that she has the intimate details of my time with her brother, but at least she knew the story before he appeared back into my life.

"Mom, I need you to remain calm and not scream or cry. You have to be quiet when I show you what I'm about to show you," he says. I hear Hazel's bedroom door open.

His voice trails off, and that won't do. I need to hear her response.

As quietly as possible, I open the bedroom door and sneak out into the hall and stand just outside Hazel's door.

"Mom, I'd like for you to meet your granddaughter. Her name is Hazel."

The sound of a female gasp hits my ears. "Trevin, explain that gorgeous little girl to me," his mom says, her voice cracking.

"Cadence, that's her mom. She and I met over a year ago. It was a night I'll never forget, and it gave us Hazel."

"Your dream girl?" she asks. My eyes widen at his mother's knowledge of our night together.

"That's her."

"How did you find her? Does she know that you looked for her? Oh, honey," his mom murmurs.

"I'm moving home, Ma," he says. "I need to be here for my girls." Butterflies take flight, and emotion clogs my throat. It's as if it's real now that he's telling his mother.

"What about your job?"

"I'm going to call Grant Riggins on Monday and tell him. Maybe they have a spot here for me at the Indy location? I'm not sure, and right now, I can't find it in me to care. I can't walk away from them. I won't." There's conviction in his voice that threatens to take my breath away.

I wipe the tears from my eyes and slide to the floor, burying my face in my hands. It's too much. Too many emotions are running through me. Regret that I ran scared, happiness for my daughter who has a father who loves her and is willing to uproot his life to be with her, and then there is this flutter in my chest that's always there when I think about him. The him from my past, and the him from the present. I feel this deep-rooted connection with him that scares the hell out of me. I've never had someone who stuck around. No one except for Shelby, and well, Thea if you count the last year.

My head jerks up when I feel his hand on my shoulder. Trevin is crouching in front of me, a look of worry on his handsome face. "Baby, what's wrong?"

"Nothing." I smile, wiping at my cheeks.

"It's something."

"You're really moving here?"

"Of course, I am. I told you that."

"I know, but I—" I stop speaking. He doesn't need me to lay my shit life on him right now.

"Come on." He stands and offers me his hand. I take it and let him pull me to my feet. He leads us into my bedroom and motions for me to climb into bed. Too exhausted to argue, I do as he asks. "Now, tell me. Don't hold back with me, Cadence. We know what happens when we do that. Nothing but truth between us from here on out. Tell me what's on your mind."

"I lost my parents when I was young. Well, my mom. I guess my dad was never around, at least that's what I've read in my file. My mom was addicted to drugs. She overdosed when I was six. I went into the foster care system, and was bounced around from home to home. When I was about nine I landed with a family that stuck. They were good to me, but not overly loving. They made sure I had food, clean clothes that fit, and everything I needed, they were just emotionally detached. When I turned eighteen, they allowed me to stay with them until I could move into my college dorm and that was it. Shelby, my best friend, was my roommate my freshman year and we've been close ever since. She's been my person until I met Thea when I moved here about a year ago."

"I'm sorry," he says softly.

"I don't want you to be sorry for me. I just— To hear you say you're staying and then tell your mom the same thing, it just kind of hit me that Hazel is going to have both parents. That you're a man of your word, and that she's not going to grow up like I did. She's going to have two parents who love her, an aunt who she already adores, and grandparents," I say, choking on the word. "She's going to have a real family. Something I never had."

"It's not just her, Cadence. It's you too. You're her mother. My family is your family. *You're* my family." He leans in close and kisses the corner of my mouth. "I'm not letting you leave me again," he says, pulling me into his arms.

We lie together, holding onto one another as his words filter through my mind. I know we need to start getting ready for the day, but I never want to leave his arms, or this apartment where, for the time being, he's not just a memory, he's all mine.

*All ours.*

## CHAPTER 8

Trevin

It's Sunday night at six, and I'm still in Indianapolis. I have a long three hours' drive back to Lexington, but I can't seem to make moves to go. I hate the thought of leaving here, leaving them. It's pulling at my heart, and I hate it.

"Don't you need to get on the road?" Scott asks.

"Yeah," I agree, not taking my eyes off Cadence and Hazel, where they sit on the couch with my sister and nephew, Clint.

"I can't believe Cadence is your dream girl." He smiles. "It's a small world. At least now I know it wasn't just some drunken dream," he comments.

"Hey." I turn to face him.

"There he is. Now I have your attention."

"I don't want to leave them here."

"They're going to be just fine. I'm next door, and I've been watching out for her since the moment my wife declared Cadence as her new bestie."

"It's my job," I say, irritated and thankful at the same time that my best friend has been looking out for my family.

*My family.*

"Maybe I can convince her to come with me?"

"Nah, she's got a good job, which she never misses unless it's for Hazel. She saves all of her time off for that little girl."

"She's a good mom."

"She is."

"I'm in love with her." I see him nod from the corner of my eye.

"Figured as much."

"It's crazy, right? One night, and then this weekend, and my heart feels as though it could explode from how much I feel for her."

"Is it maybe just because she's the mother of your daughter? And by the way, no paternity test?"

"No. She's mine. I feel it."

"She looks like you. I don't know how Thea and I didn't put it together before now. Well, I do. I knew about your dream girl, and so did Thea."

"Yeah, thanks for that," I say to him, but he keeps going.

"She also knew about Cadence's situation. I'm shocked she didn't put two and two together."

"She probably would have, but I never told you where I was when I met her. I didn't tell you it was my last visit."

"That's probably it. You know my wife, if she even suspected, she would have been all over that like a rat on a Cheeto."

"I do know *my* sister, and you're right. She would have been," I agree. Cadence and I both have regrets from that night. We both have to live with them, and move forward. That's exactly what I plan to do. Move forward as a family.

Leaving him, I go to my girls, lowering myself to the floor to sit next to them. I offer Hazel my finger, which she latches onto immediately.

"Are you ready to go?" Cadence asks.

"No."

"You have a three-hour drive," Thea reminds me.

"I know. I'm not going."

"What do you mean you're not going?" my sister asks.

I ignore her and look to Cadence. "I can't make myself leave the two of you." I hear my sister say "aww," but I continue to ignore her. "Do you think you can take a day or two off and come with me?"

"I don't know. I save that time in case Hazel gets sick."

"You're not doing it all on your own anymore, Cadence. You have me, and I promise you I'll be there for every minute. Please?" I'm aware of the pleading in my voice, and I'm not the least bit ashamed, not when it comes to my girls. I'll do what it takes.

"Babe, have you seen my phone? I need to record this. Trevin Hubbard is begging." Scott chuckles.

Raising my hand in the air, I flip him off, making him laugh. Hazel turns to look at me, and I move to take her from Cadence. "Hey, baby girl," I say softly. "Tell Momma you want to take a road trip with Daddy," I tell my daughter. She just smiles and coos. "See, babe. She wants to go."

"I can't just call in, Trevin."

"How much time do you need?"

She's quiet so long I think she's going to flat out turn me down. I'm surprised when she pulls out her phone and taps the screen before putting it to her ear. "Hi, Debbie, this is Cadence. Something has come up, and I was hoping to take a few days off. I know I have patients scheduled, but—" She stops and listens. "Really? Are you sure? Thank you so much, Debbie. I'll be back on Monday." She hangs up and looks at me. "That was my boss. It turns out she was going to offer me some time off this week. There's a new therapist starting, and she wants her to take my schedule for the week, while Debbie works with her to show her the ropes."

"Why not just have you train her?" Thea asks.

"Debbie likes to get firsthand knowledge of how her new hires are with patients. She always trains herself. The last time she did this, I got caught up on charting and did some continuing education classes."

"You said Monday."

"Yeah, I'm free this entire week." I don't even try to hide my smile. My girls are coming home with me, which means I don't have to be without them. I've already missed so much time, the thought of leaving them even temporarily was tearing me in two.

"Come here." I motion for her to lean closer. As soon as her lips are close enough, I kiss her, not giving a damn that we have an audience. "You're coming home with me?"

"For a few days."

"That's all I need. Come on." I manage to stand, still holding Hazel. "We need to pack what she's going to need for the week. I read that it's best to travel when babies are sleeping to not interrupt their routine. If we leave here around eight, we can make it to my place at eleven, feed her, and maybe she'll sleep for the rest of the night."

"You read? Why have you been reading about babies?" Scott asks.

"Because I'm a father."

"When?" Thea asks.

"While my girls were sleeping the past two nights."

"Trevin," Cadence whispers. I can see the wonder in her eyes, and the disbelief. I don't care how long it takes, I'm going to prove to her that I'm in this. That she and our daughter are my world. I know it's fast, but when you know, you know, and I am certain that she is who I want. I want us to raise our daughter together, and have more babies that I'll be there for every step of the way.

"I needed to know what to expect, how to take care of Hazel, and help you. You've had the entire pregnancy and the first three months of her life to get up to speed. I had some catching up to do. I still have some catching up to do."

Cadence nods, leaning in and pressing her lips to mine. "You're one of a kind, Trevin Hubbard. I'm so glad we found our way back."

"Me too, baby. Me too." My voice is thick, and I'm man enough to admit I'm choked up. I went from wondering if I had imagined her and our night together, to having a family. I'll take the latter every damn time.

"You better get moving," Thea says. I can hear the tears in her voice, and sure enough, when I glance at my sister, she's wiping at her cheeks as Scott takes their son into his arms.

"Hear that, baby girl?" I ask Hazel. "You get to come home with Daddy for a few days." I'm already imagining them in my space. Sure it's not where we're going to be living, but having them in my home, it's going to make this all that much more real.

"Call me when you get there," Thea says.

"We will," Cadence assures her.

I stand with Hazel in my arms, offering Cadence my hand. We say a quick goodbye before heading across the hall to pack.

\*\*\*

"For such a tiny thing, she sure needs a lot," I say as I carry in the final bag.

"Well, she needed the Pack 'n Play to have a safe place to sleep. Bottles, diapers, formula, clothes, blankets, toys." Cadence stops and begins to laugh. "She does have a lot. I've never gone anywhere except to Thea's or to visit Shelby for a few hours or to the doctor's office. This is a first for me."

"Well, we're going to need to find a bigger place. She's already overrunning your apartment, and when we have more, it's going to get worse. Besides, there are only two bedrooms."

"We? A bigger house?" she asks.

"Yeah, we're doing this, right? You, me, and Hazel?" I study her hard and see the tears well in her eyes.

Slowly, she nods. "Y-Yes. We're doing this."

"Good. Now, let me figure out how to set this thing up in my room, and we'll get her fed and changed and back into bed."

"Let's just set up the Pack 'n Play and try to lay her down. She might sleep a little longer."

"Okay. Well, here goes nothing."

"You watch her, and I'll put it up."

"I need to learn how to do it," I tell her.

"It's easy. It just pops open. Show me where to set it up."

Picking up Hazel's car seat which she's snoozing in, I lead Cadence to my bedroom. "In the corner, maybe?"

"That should be fine." Cadence wastes no time getting to work setting up the Pack 'n Play, and I watch, making sure I see how she does it. I don't want to be the dad who never does a damn thing for his kid. We made her together. We're going to take care of her together. That's how my parents raised Thea and me, and that's how I plan for us to raise Hazel.

*Together.*

"You want to try, or do you want me to?" Cadence points to our sleeping daughter.

"I'll do it." I set the seat on the bed and slowly unclasp the straps. Well, I try to. "What is this, some kind of torture device?" I ask Cadence, making her laugh.

"Let me show you." She moves in close, and I step back, letting her do her thing. My hands rest on her hips. She's standing in front of me, with me looking over her shoulder, watching her as she expertly unclasps the straps and lifts our sleeping daughter. Hazel's little body stretches, but she doesn't wake up, not even when Cadence lays her back down. "She'll sleep for a few more hours."

"Okay. Well, let's make sure we have everything we might need unpacked for when she does, and we can lie down and try to get some sleep too."

"Everything we should need is going to be in the diaper bag. I made sure it was well packed before we left."

"Perfect. T-shirts are in the top drawer. I'm going to go lock up. Need anything?"

"No." She shakes her head.

"I'll be right back." With a quick kiss to her lips, I leave my room to lock up the house. I find myself checking all the doors twice, and even the windows. I have two ladies to protect, and I take that shit seriously. Satisfied that the house is secure, I grab two bottles of water from the fridge and, in the dark, make my way to my room.

"Is this okay?" she asks, looking down at the old concert T-shirt of mine that's covering what I know is the sexiest body I'll ever lay eyes on.

"You're perfect." I place one of the bottles of water on

the nightstand next to where she's standing and walk around the bed, peeking in on Hazel before stripping down to my underwear. I take a drink of water and turn to Cadence. "Do we need to keep the lamp on for her?"

"No, she'll be fine in the dark."

"What about you?"

"You're here to protect me, right?" she teases.

"Always." I switch off the lamp and crawl under the covers. The bed dips when she does the same, and I waste no time moving over and pulling her into my arms. "Night, baby."

"Night, Trevin."

I'm exhausted from the drive and the two previous sleepless nights. With both of my girls here with me, though, it takes no amount of time for sleep to claim me.

# CHAPTER 9

Cadence

We've been at Trevin's place in Lexington for four days, and the time has been nothing short of amazing. He's had to go into the office each day while Hazel and I hang out at the house. He brought boxes home the first day and asked me if I minded helping him pack. That's when it hits me that this is really happening. He's moving back to Indianapolis. He's going to be a constant in our lives.

"Honey, I'm home," Trevin calls out. I don't bother to hide my smile when he walks into the living room where Hazel and I are spread out on a blanket on the living room floor. "I missed you." He settles on the other side of Hazel, leaning over her to kiss me, then dropping a kiss to her forehead. "What did my girls do today?"

"The kitchen is packed, and it wore us out, huh, Hazel?" I ask like my daughter is actually going to respond.

"Thank you for doing that. I know it's a lot to ask of you when you're also taking care of her."

"It's no problem. I did most of it while she was napping. How was work?"

"Well, we got it all figured out. I'll be transferring to the Indy plant. I'm going to be the new assistant plant manager. It's a small pay cut, but that's okay. It gets me home with my family, and I love working for Riggins Enterprises. It's the best of both worlds. Not to mention, Harold, the current plant manager, is talking about retiring next year. I had a meeting with Royce and Grant today, and they've assured me that the position is mine when that happens."

"Are you sure this is what you want?" I know I sound like a broken record. I've asked him this same question every day since we've been here. This is all happening so fast. I just want to make sure this is truly what he wants.

"Positive. I was prepared to leave Riggins Enterprises all together. Luckily, I don't have to. They're a great company to work for, and they've been good to me. I get my girls, I get to move closer to my parents and my sister, and I get to keep working for them. I couldn't think of a better scenario."

There's an ease in my shoulders, as though a weight has been lifted. "I know this is a lot for you, but I'm so grateful you're going to be in her life."

"It's not just her, Cadence. It's you too. I want a life with you. I want us to be a family." He pauses, letting his words sink in. "I know we've not really talked about us, we've kept it all about me moving to be closer to Hazel, but, babe, it's not just her I want to be closer to. It's you too."

Tears burn my eyes as they threaten to fall. I open my mouth to speak, but no words come, so instead, I give him a watery smile and nod. "O-kay." I manage to push the words out after swallowing back the lump in my throat.

"Although I think we're going to need a bigger place. I don't see all of my stuff fitting in your small apartment."

"You're probably right," I say with a smile.

"I'll start looking for houses. We'll need to research the schools and surroundings areas. It's going to take us some time. Plus, we want it to be a convenient distance to both of our jobs."

"You're buying a house?" My heart stammers in my chest. Is this really happening? Every dream I've ever had for Hazel and me, to find him one day, is finally happening.

"No. *We're* buying a house," he corrects me. "It's going to be our home, Cadence. All three of us."

The words *I love you* burn on the tip of my tongue. It's crazy to even think about saying that to him, but he gave me Hazel. He gave me the most incredible gift in this life and a night that I know I will never forget. He's handing me my dreams—for me and my daughter—on a silver platter, and my heart is full. Each night after we put Hazel to bed, he makes love to me. I feel our connection in my bones, and he's so tender, so gentle, it couldn't be described as anything else.

"Since the kitchen is packed, how about we go out to eat?" he suggests.

"Order in?" I motion to my short shorts and an old T-shirt. "I'm not really dressed to go out."

"Whatever you want." He leans over and kisses me. His tongue slides past my lips as he deepens the kiss. I lean in too, wanting more of him, but tiny hands tugging at my hair have me pulling back and yelping in pain.

"No, no, sweet girl," Trevin coos. "That hurts Mommy. We don't pull hair," he tells her. "You good?"

"I'm fine. Not the first time, and I'm sure not the last." I tap Hazel's nose with my index finger. "This one has an iron grip."

"Any preference for dinner?"

"Nope. Surprise me. I'm going to take this little one and give her a bath."

"I'm going to order, and I'll be up to help." He bends to give Hazel a kiss on her cheek, and then a little further pressing his lips to mine.

"All right, little lady. It's time for your bath." Before I can lift her off the floor, Trevin is on his feet and taking her with him.

"Did you grow today while Daddy was gone?" He lifts her into the air over his head, and she babbles like she always does when she's the center of her daddy's attention. He blows a raspberry on her belly, where her shirt has ridden up, and her tiny hands fist his hair, making him laugh. "All right, baby girl. We need to work on that," he tells her with a smile. "Go to Momma so I can order us some food." He kisses her cheek once more and places her in my arms. "I'll be right there," he says, kissing me too.

I stand still and watch him walk toward the kitchen. I can't believe this is my life, that everything I ever dreamed of is coming true.

I have a family.

"We love Daddy, don't we, Hazel?" I whisper to my daughter as I turn and head to the bathroom to give her a bath.

I've barely gotten her undressed when Trevin appears beside me. "I ordered Mexican. It will be here in about thirty minutes."

"Perfect. That gives us enough time to get her bathed and into some pajamas." I place her in the small bathtub that we had to buy because, of course, I forgot to pack it. Together we sit on the floor beside the tub that holds her baby tub and give our daughter a bath. This has become our routine. I tell him he doesn't have to help, but he claims he doesn't want to miss another moment of her life. I melt into a puddle every time he says things like that, which is pretty much any time he's talking.

"Trev?"

"Yeah?" he asks, lifting Hazel from the tub and wrapping her in a towel.

"I'm glad it was you. I'm glad you were my first, and that this situation—" I motion between the three of us. "I wouldn't want it to be anyone else."

His eyes soften. "Hazel, Mommy's making Daddy soft." My eyes dart to his crotch, and he is most definitely not soft. "In here." He taps his free hand that's not holding our daughter over his heart. "There will never be an issue with soft there." He looks down at his crotch and back up to me. "Not where you're concerned." Those hazel eyes of his show me that he means what he says.

The doorbell rings, and he smirks. "That's dinner." He stands, our daughter wrapped up in a thick towel and heads to the door. "Oh, Cadence?"

"Y-Yeah?" I reply.

"You're dessert." With that, he leaves me kneeling next to the tub on the bathroom floor, aching for him. I love my daughter, but I can't help but hope she goes to sleep with ease this evening. Her daddy promised me dessert.

## CHAPTER 10

Trevin

It's been a month since I moved back home to Indy, and there has not been a single day that I've regretted my decision. I get to fall asleep with Cadence in my arms and wake up the same way. I get to hold my daughter, give her baths, and read her stories while her momma feeds her at night. I get to hold both of my girls in my arms, and there is nothing more in this world I could ask for.

Well, maybe one thing. A bigger house. This two-bedroom is cramped with the three of us. I have most of my things in storage. We've been looking at houses, but nothing has jumped out at us as being the one. Not to mention, we still have my house in Lexington on the market. As soon as we get that sold, we'll have more flexibility with what we can purchase. I want a home. I want the big yard and plenty of space for our growing family. I want Hazel to feel settled, safe, and secure, just like Thea and I were as kids.

Not just Hazel, but Cadence too. There is a pain in my

chest anytime I let myself think about how she grew up. I want her to have everything she's missed out on, everything she's ever dreamed of. I won't stop until I do. That's what you do when you love someone.

*And I love her.*

Not just because she's the mother of my child, I love her spirit. I love coming home to her, and I love knowing that we're a team. I could sit here for hours and list off items that make me love her and fall harder every day. However, I don't need to. I know it's her. It's who she is as a person.

Raising my hand to knock on my sister's door, it opens before I get the chance. "Hey," Scott greets me. "You're home early."

"So are you."

"Yeah." He grins.

"What's going on?"

He looks over his shoulder and pulls the door shut. "Nothing, I came home early, that's all."

"You do remember we've been best friends since kindergarten, right?"

"Fuck. You can't tell her I told you," he says. There's a smile on his face, and he runs his hands through his hair. A sign he's excited or nervous.

"Spill it."

"We're pregnant." I swear I've only ever seen him smile like he is now when it comes to my baby sister.

"Congrats, man." I give him a half hug.

"Thanks. We weren't trying, but fuck, man, I'm stoked."

"Spare me the details of how my nieces and nephews get here," I joke.

"We need a bigger place."

"I know that feeling. We've been looking," I say as my phone rings. "Hello."

"Mr. Hubbard, this is Alice from Lexington Realty. I wanted to let you know I sent an offer to your email. Full asking," she says excitedly.

"Perfect. I'm picking up my daughter now. I'll log in as soon as I can and sign it."

"That sounds like a plan. I'll be in touch."

"Thanks, Alice."

"Good news?"

"Yeah. I sold my place in Lexington. Full asking."

"Congrats, man."

"Thanks. I'm going to get Hazel, and you and my sister can celebrate. You want me to take Clint to our place?"

"Nah. I want him close."

I nod because I know how he feels. No matter how much time I spend with my girls, it's never enough. "If you change your mind, let me know."

"Thanks, man." He opens the door, and I follow him inside their apartment.

"Hey, you're early," Thea says from her spot on the couch. She has Hazel in her arms and Clint sitting next to her. Both kids are sound asleep.

"Looks like Aunt Thea has the magic touch."

Her eyes flash to Scott. "Something like that."

My sister is glowing, much like my best friend. "I'll take her." I gently lift Hazel from her lap and cuddle her in my arms, pulling in her baby scent. If you would have told me a year ago I'd be sniffing babies and finding comfort in that, I would have told you that you've lost your damn mind. Now? Now, it's what I crave.

"Everything okay? You're never home this early."

"Yeah, it's all good. Cadence works late tonight. I decided to come home and get this little one bathed and in her jammies and have dinner ready when she gets home.

That way, we can have our family time before Hazel has to go to sleep."

"Aww," Thea says, her eyes welling with tears. "I love the way you love them."

"Nothing in life is worth doing halfway." I wink at Thea, give Scott a nod, and gather Hazel's things. "Thanks, sis."

"You're welcome."

"Hey, we're looking to move. We want you to keep watching her if you're interested."

"Definitely."

"We're looking too," Scott adds.

I nod. "Well, maybe we should discuss locations. We can maybe buy in the same area for convenience."

"Good schools are a must," Thea says.

"We agree with that. Nothing has to be decided now. I just wanted you to know we're looking but want you to continue to watch her. The thought of a stranger keeping her doesn't sit well with me."

"We feel the same way."

"Thanks. We'll see you in the morning." I wave to them and head across the hall to our apartment. Since Hazel is still sleeping soundly, I pick up the living room, unload the dishwasher, and start a load of laundry. Thankfully this apartment complex offers a small closet in each unit for a laundry room. I'm just finishing tossing the first load into the dryer and starting a second when Hazel wakes up. We go through the routine of giving her a bottle and reading a couple of books. She's so still in my arms as I read to her.

"It's time to start on dinner," I tell her. "We're going to set you up in your swing while Daddy gets lasagna in the oven." I chatter to Hazel the entire time I'm cooking, and she babbles right back. I love every second of my time with her.

"Now that that's done, it's time for you, Miss Stinky Butt, to get a bath." I pick her up and fly her through the house like an airplane, and she laughs. Her little baby giggles are the best sound on this earth. Bath time is fun. The older she gets, the more splashing and playing she does.

I'm zipping up her pajamas when I hear Cadence's keys in the front door. "Mommy's home," I tell Hazel, lifting her from the changing table into my arms.

"What's going on?" Cadence asks.

"Dinner is almost ready, and this one just got her bath."

"How did you manage to do all of this? I'm only, what, an hour later than usual?"

"I left the office early. I know you've had a long week with your patient load, and I wanted to take some of this off your plate. I know you've been missing your snuggle time with dinner and bath each night getting home later, so we did it all before you got here." I step toward her and slide my arm around her waist, pulling her into me and kissing her softly. "Sit. I'll make you a plate." Hazel is already reaching for her mom, so we make the switch, and I turn to walk away.

"Trev?" she calls out. There's a quiver in her voice.

"Yeah?"

"I love you."

The room stills, but my heart keeps on beating like a bass drum in my chest. In two long strides, I'm standing in front of her. Cradling her face in the palm of my hands, I stare into her eyes. "I love you. So fucking much," I say, kissing her.

I take my time tasting her, showing her with my kiss how much she means to me. Pulling out of the kiss, I press my forehead against hers. We both laugh when Hazel mimics us. "I love you too," I tell our daughter.

I've been waiting for the perfect time to tell her, and this moment, it's another one to add to my long list of unforgettable. That's how it should be. Every other memory is them. My girls and I wouldn't want it any other way.

# EPILOGUE CADENCE

Cadence

"Come here, you little bugger." I run after my daughter, who is crawling all over the place, and scoop her into my arms.

"She likes the extra space." Trevin laughs.

"This is overkill, Trevin. Why do we need a five-bedroom house?"

"For the kids?"

"We have one kid."

"But we're going to have more. Trust me. We've been practicing. I think the odds are in our favor." He smirks.

He's not wrong. It's been six months since the day I walked into Thea and Scott's apartment and saw him holding our daughter. Six months of happiness and love. So much love. We've been living in my two-bedroom apartment until today, when Trevin and I signed the loan papers to purchase our first house. We have been looking for a while, and nothing screamed home to us. Not until we found this place. It just so happens to be only two miles from the house that Scott and Thea moved into two months ago. They wasted no time purchasing a bigger place when they learned they would be adding to their family. He wanted a house. Hell, he wanted to buy one as soon as he moved back to town. It was my insistence that we take some time before jumping into anything that kept him from it. As soon as his house in Lexington sold, he was a man on a mission. We looked at maybe a couple of dozen before deciding on this one. I thought it was too big. Trev said it was perfect. I admit it's gorgeous, but it's huge compared to our apartment.

"Just wait until she starts walking. Scott was telling me how Clint is into everything these days. They found him on the bathroom sink covered in shaving cream the other day." Trevin laughs.

"Stop," I tell him, barely containing my own laughter. "You're going to jinx us."

"No way, not our angel," he says, taking Hazel from my arms. He blows on her belly, making her cackle with laughter.

"Where do we start?" I ask, looking around at all the boxes.

"One box at a time. We're both off this week, and Thea said she would keep Hazel even though we're not working, so we can bust it all out. However, right now, I want to show you something."

He holds his hand out for me and leads me down the hall toward the first-floor master suite. Pushing open the door, he motions for me to walk in first. When I step into the room, I gasp at what I see. There are hundreds if not thousands of rose petals spread out on the gray hardwood floor. Candles, which appear to be operating on batteries instead of actual flames, are placed around the room as well.

I turn to look at him and find him kneeling on the floor, Hazel still on his hip. "Mommy, we love you," he says, glancing down at Hazel. "You take care of us and have given us, given *me* my reason for living. I can't imagine my life without either of my girls. What do you say we make this forever thing official? We want you to be a Hubbard with us," he says, as he offers an open tiny blue box, with a diamond ring sparkling at me.

I don't need to think about it. "Yes." I walk to where they are and kneel with them. He places Hazel on the floor, and she crawls away.

"That's why I chose the battery candles." He shakes his head, watching our daughter before turning those hazel eyes on me. His lips capture mine, and time seems to stand still as I process the fact that this man just asked me to marry him.

"We're getting married," I murmur against his lips.

The smile he gives me lights up his face. Pulling the ring out of the box, he slides it on my finger. "I love you, future Mrs. Hubbard."

"I love you too."

He looks around me to check on Hazel. "No, baby girl. We don't eat flowers," he says, standing to grab her and take the rose petal she was trying to shove into her mouth.

I smile at them and look back at my ring.

A lifetime of this is exactly what I want. Trevin is no longer a memory; he's my heart, and he's my future.

# EPILOGUE TREVIN

Trevin

Five years later

As I sit here on the back deck, nursing a beer holding my son, I can't help but reflect on my life. A chance meeting at a club. An attraction that was undeniable led me here to where I am today. Hazel cackles with laughter as Cadence chases after her, our middle daughter Violet doing her best to catch up with them.

Cadence drops to her knees in a pile of leaves, our daughters doing the same and their laughter of my girls fills my heart. Connor stretches his little arms and legs, but stays resting against my chest. He'll be three weeks old tomorrow. I missed all the pregnancy moments with Hazel, so when we found out we were pregnant with Violet, I made sure I didn't miss a single second. Nothing changed when we found out we were pregnant with our little man. There is nothing better in this life than watching the woman you love grow with a child that the two of you created out of the love that you share.

*Nothing better.*

The fall leaves blow through the air, and as the sun begins to set, I know I need to get Connor inside. Standing, I grab my half-empty bottle of beer to do just that, but the Hubbard girls race to the back deck, and two sets of little arms are wrapping around my legs.

"Hey, handsome." Cadence rises on her toes and kisses me. "I see he's still snoozing."

"He is." She places her hand over mine that's resting on Connor's back.

"Daddy, can we have a piggyback ride? Please?" Hazel asks.

"Pwease?" Violet, at three, mocks her older sister.

"Hand him over, Hubbard. You know you can't resist them."

"It's not just them I can't resist." I bend down and kiss her again. No matter how many times my lips are pressed against hers, it will never be enough. Not in this lifetime, and not the next. I crave her.

"Eww, Daddy, stop kissing Mommy." Hazel pulls on my jeans.

"Oh, I think someone needs the tickle monster after that." The words barely leave my mouth before my daughters are screeching with pure joy and racing into the house to hide.

"I love you, Trevin Hubbard."

"I love you too, Mrs. Hubbard."

## THANK YOU

Thank you for taking the time to read Every Other Memory.

* * *

***Never miss a new release:*** Newsletter Sign-up Be the first to hear about free content, new releases, cover reveals, sales, and more.

* * *

Discover more about Kaylee's books here.

* * *

Start the Riggins Brothers Series for FREE. Download Play by Play now.

* * *

Contact Kaylee Ryan:
- **Website**
- **Facebook**
- **Instagram**
- **Reader Group**
- **Goodreads**
- **BookBub**

## MORE FROM KAYLEE RYAN

***With You Series:***
*Anywhere with You | More with You*
*Everything with You*

***Soul Serenade Series***:
*Emphatic | Assured*
*Definite | Insistent*

***Southern Heart Series:***
*Southern Pleasure | Southern Desire*
*Southern Attraction | Southern Devotion*

***Unexpected Arrivals Series***
*Unexpected Reality |Unexpected Fight*
*Unexpected Fall | Unexpected Bond*
*Unexpected Odds*

***Riggins Brothers Series:***

*Play by Play / Layer by Layer*
*Piece by Piece / Kiss by Kiss*
*Touch by Touch | Beat by Beat*

### *Standalone Titles:*
*Tempting Tatum | Unwrapping Tatum | Levitate*
*Just Say When | I Just Want You*
*Reminding Avery*
*Hey, Whiskey*
*Pull You Through | Beyond the Bases*
*Remedy | The Difference*
*Trust the Push | Forever After All*

### *Entangled Hearts Duet:*
*Agony | Bliss*

### *Cocky Hero Club:*
*Lucky Bastard*

### *Mason Creek Series:*
*Perfect Embrace*

Box Sets*:*
*Series Starter - Kaylee Ryan*

### **Co-written with Lacey Black:**

### *Fair Lakes Series:*
*It's Not Over | Just Getting Started*
*Can't Fight It*

***Standalone Titles:***
*Boy Trouble*
*Home to You*
*Beneath the Fallen Stars*

Printed in Great Britain
by Amazon